SAVAGE VENGEANCE

Lorelei stood away from Gunn, looked him up and down. He felt her scathing glance, tried a wry smile. It didn't work. Her expression grew serious. She did have a point to make. He knew that.

"You look like a man who can handle himself. You've got a good horse, a pistol. A Winchester rifle. Yet, you did nothing to save my father. You watched him being shot down and you never tried to help."

Gunn reached for her. She was cracking. Her voice quavered. She was on the verge of hysteria. Tears welled up in her eyes. She pushed him away. He felt the hurt like a stab in the heart. He reached out for her again, but she backed away, her eyes glittering with a savage light.

And in her hands was his Colt .45. . . .

THE HOTTEST SERIES IN THE WEST CONTINUES!

GUNN #14: THE BUFF RUNNERS (1093, $2.25)

Gunn runs into two hell-raising sisters caught in the middle of a buffalo hunter's feud. He hires out his sharpshooting skills—and doubles their fun!

GUNN #15: DRYGULCHED (1142, $2.25)

When Gunn agrees to look after a dying man's two lovely daughters, he finds himself having to solve a poaching problem too. And he's going to have to bring peace to the mountains—before he can get any himself!

GUNN #16: WYOMING WANTON (1196, $2.25)

Wrongly accused of murder, Gunn needs a place to lay low and plan his proof of innocence. And—when the next body turns up—pretty Mary is his only alibi. But will she lay her reputation on the line for Gunn?

GUNN #17: TUCSON TWOSOME (1236, $2.25)

Hard-ridin' Gunn finds himself dead center . . . the target of the Apaches, the Cavalry, and the luscious Tucson Twosome—and everyone wants a piece of Gunn's action!

GUNN #18: THE GOLDEN LADY (1298, $2.25)

Gunn's got a beautiful miner's daughter in front of him, and hard-case killers closing in on him from the rear. It looks like he'll be shooting in all directions!

THE GOLDEN LADY #18
GUNN

BY JORY SHERMAN

ZEBRA BOOKS
KENSINGTON PUBLISHING CORP.

ZEBRA BOOKS

are published by

KENSINGTON PUBLISHING CORP.
475 Park Avenue South
New York, N.Y. 10016

First printing: December, 1983

Printed in the United States of America

For Bob Randisi, a smith of both guns and words.

CHAPTER ONE

A man can die so easy.

A man can die from trying too hard. A man can die from being in the wrong place at the wrong time.

A man can die from just thinking about death.

He can die from grief, from heartbreak, from loneliness.

And a man can die from disease, starvation and thirst.

William Gunnison, the man they called Gunn, was dying.

The fluids in his body had been sucked out by the sun and the wind. The water he had drunk at the last well had been no more than a half cupful, and to dig for it a man would die just from the effort. His hands would blister and his heart would stop pumping as his blood turned to dust.

But a man like Gunn doesn't give up.

He sat the saddle and felt his butt bones ram up into his spine. He ran a dry tongue over cracked lips caked with the sour acid of earth and he knew the blindness of a man going insane when there was no shade and no end to the road.

Lakes danced before his eyes.

Shimmering waters beckoned, only to fade away like smoke wisps. He could not speak beyond a croak and he heard the lovely sounds of women's voices speaking to him, calling his name.

Gunn was not ready to die and his horse kept going, although its master swayed half-delirious in the saddle.

And then it happened.

The sound. A real sound. Not something his seared brain had imagined.

The sound startled him.

After the long silent miles, the groan and creak of wood was a surprise. The sound was monotonous, irritating, the screech reminding him of something out of Kansas or Nebraska. But this was as far west as he had been and he'd seen no sign of life across the desert. The water in the inland salt sea had been unfit to drink and these pine-studded hills were the first relief in a long, hot journey from Fort Yuma. There had been water-holes rimmed with alkali, poison. There had been dry holes. There had been hells.

Pines? Trees?

Gunn jerked himself out of his stupor. He was climbing, away from the desert with its Gilas, its alkali wells, its bleached bones. The air would be sweet soon. He would find water. He would live.

The sound, though, was horrible.

Worse than the sound was now had been the wind, the heat.

The wind blew hard on the land, carrying the heat, smothering him with its merciless breath.

Grit and dust stung Gunn's eyes. The sand lashed his lean face, gouged at the velvety inner lining of his eyes. Pale gray eyes that hurt, that burned like fire.

He looked around, realized that he must have been climbing for some time. Climbing, up, away from the blazing desert, into a high country that he had not seen through grit-raked eyes, through his thirst-crazed insanity.

The land below still boiled into a shadow cloud of dust that blotted out his trail, left him stranded in the hills, lost and weary, burning with a fever that cracked his lips, made his throat ache for anything wetter than dry sand.

Even here, on high ground, the fire ate at him, dulled his senses so that he could not be sure if he had heard the sound or only imagined it.

The fire stayed with him. A fire of dust that seemed to linger on his clothes, his skin. A fire of baked earth reflecting the heat upward into his face like the blast from a furnace.

The tall, gray-eyed man was dry and his canteen empty. He had not quenched his thirst in forty miles and now he could taste water, even on the arid, gritty wind. That noise was man-made. It didn't come from trees or rocks, but from something that sounded familiar.

Gunn ticked single-studded spurs into his horse Esquire's flanks, urging the Tennessee walker up the rise in the direction of the sound. A machine that made a noise like that meant water, or ought to, and who could refuse a man water in this country? The trail was rutted from use, wide enough for a single wagon, the best road he'd seen since crossing the Anza-Borrego.

And now he could see the trail ahead. The pines soaked up the dust, gave him a windbreak.

Horse and man topped the rise and Gunn saw what was making the sound. The sun glinted off the wooden blades of the windmill. Kansas, Nebraska, just over the next hill. The blades spun wildly in the updrafts, the shaft, twisting to catch every zephyr, needed oiling. The sound grated on a man's nerves.

The gunshot drowned out the sound of the creaking windmill shaft, broke the monontony of the groaning stavelike blades whirling at high speed. Gunn hauled back on the reins, instinctively reached for his sidearm, a Colt single-action .45 Peacemaker. A bullet whined somewhere below him. The hackles rose on the back of his neck.

Two more gunshots boomed. And another. Two men, three.

Target practice?

"Steady, boy," said Gunn, his gray-blue eyes narrowing. Esquire pranced in place, bowing his neck, mouthing the bit.

A choice to be made. Ride over the hill in the direction of the gunfire hoping it was just a bunch funning, ride wide and ride on, or dismount and approach slowly, rifle in hand. Gunn held Esquire back, knowing the horse smelled water and danger as well.

The big sorrel with the flax mane and tail and four white stockings backed down, but the bit was digging into his mouth.

"Damnit, 'Squire, settle down."

Gunn's decision came easy after he heard the shouts.

10

"Get the hell off'n my property, Chigger!"

Followed by a gunshot, the whine of a bullet scorching the air.

"Snake, I got a bullet fer you, too."

Gunn heard the explosion, winced as the bullet sizzled overhead. Whoever was yelling was a wild shot. A man could get killed just sitting there burning to death in the sun.

The tall, lean man dismounted, tied Esquire's reins to a stunted tree growing out of the rocks.

A fusillade blasted the silence. The explosions echoed. A bullet ricocheted off a rock with an eerie whine.

Gunn jerked his Winchester out of its scabbard, hunched low and headed for the top of the hill. Whoever was shooting down there wasn't funning. They were dead serious.

Quiet, then a single shot perforated the still moment when even the cranking metallic sound seemed to die down.

"Freddie, give it up," said a gruff-voiced man Gunn couldn't see.

"We got you cold, Waite." Another voice, slightly higher-pitched, a trace of a brogue in its tones.

Three men, so far. Perhaps no more. Gunn eased over the hill, stepping carefully so that his boots didn't scrape against the small stones on the side of the road. He crept toward a rock, snugged up hard behind it. He peered over the top.

There, in a small bowl of a canyon, he saw the windmill. It swung with the wind, its blades churning the dry air. Its shaft groaned and creaked with a terrible sound, an agonizing scrape of straining wood. There was a wooden stock tank nearby, a log cabin nestled up against the side of the hill. Two men on horseback rode back and forth, their paths crisscrossing. They stared at a huge black hole in the mountainside. Two mules circled restlessly in a pole corral. A buckboard stood idle near the cabin.

Gunn saw a couple of dry rockers, some tools.

He sucked in a breath, waited.

A man's head appeared out of the black hole that had been blasted into the hillside. The two men on horseback were waiting. They fired simultaneously. Sparks flew off of the cave rocks. Splinters of rock cracked off. Dust rose from the places where the lead bullets had hit.

The man in the cave, too far away for Gunn to make out his features, fired another wild shot. The bullet didn't even come close to either man riding back and forth. Now, Gunn knew why his shots were going wild. He wasn't aiming. Either he couldn't see or he was scared witless.

"The damn fool is just wasting bullets," Gunn said under his breath.

The man in the cave fired twice more and then cursed loudly. Gunn saw him shake his rifle helplessly, try to work the lever.

That's when the two men on horseback made their moves. They whipped their horses, raced toward the cave. Both men fired at point-blank range, catching their hapless prey in a merciless crossfire. The man with the broken rifle twisted as bullets plunked into his flesh. He staggered out of the cave into the blaze of light, the echoing booms of riflefire.

He fell.

Gunn croaked his outrage, felt his throat tear apart as if ripped by a cougar's claws.

One of the men dismounted, rushed into the opening. He was quick and light on his feet. The thin one. He tossed leather bags up to his partner who had ridden in close. The man, still on horseback, caught them deftly, stuck them into empty saddlebags with their flaps open.

Gunn stood up, leveled his rifle. His hand, touching the sun-scalded metal, turned to fire, as if he had touched it to a hot stove. He cursed soundlessly, managed to get a live shell into the chamber of the Winchester .44.

He yelled at the men below, "Ho!" his voice a sandpaper rasp.

And death can come to a man who sticks his nose in someone else's business.

The man on horseback wheeled, brought his rifle swinging so fast Gunn could not track its barrel. He fired.

The man on foot hollered; "Look out, Chigger, he's got a rifle!"

Gunn dove for the ground. Something told him that death was closer than the hairs of his six-day beard. The bullet fried the air over his head, singed his ears, brought up the hackles on the back of his neck. Instinctively, he rolled, knowing the man who had shot at him was no pilgrim. His stomach twisted as he realized the bullet had passed straight to where he had just stood. The lead ball cracked against a rock, ricocheted off,

13

leaving an echo like the vibrating rattles of a side-winder.

The two men fired rapidly.

Gunn, pinned down, could only snake over the hot rocky terrain and try to ignore the spatter of sand, the splintered spears of rock that slashed his skin.

And, then, it was silent.

Gunn lifted his head, saw the two men ride out of the bowl and round a bend of rock. He rose to his feet, took aim and fired. The bullet sped harmlessly into space.

The two men disappeared and only the hoofbeats of their horses echoed in their wake.

The windmill groaned on, the sound ugly now, like something alien in a graveyard. Gunn shuddered in the heat and hobbled down the slope toward the fallen man. As he drew closer, he saw the dark stain on the ground next to the stricken miner. The blood was drying in the wind. It was like walking in a graveyard.

Four paces away, Gunn heard the man groan.

"Hold on, feller," he said, rushing to the man's side. He knelt down, lay his rifle beside him.

The man's battered felt hat rolled from his head as Gunn lifted him up, cradled him in his arms. A quick examination showed he had been shot in the arm, side, and leg. The side wound was bad. Very bad.

"Water . . ."

"Too late for that. You're a goner."

The man's eyes batted open. His galluses hung from frail shoulders, caked with dust. His clothes were blood-soaked, drying quick in the heat. His breath wheezed through his throat.

"You ain't . . ."

"No. I'm not one of them. Who were they?"

"Chigger . . . Snake. Been trying to jump my claim. I—I'm Freddie Waite. Jesus."

The man's eyes closed. He shook spasmodically.

Gunn felt another bullet hole in the man's back. Through the lung. A bullet did odd things when it entered a man's body. It could go anywhere, do anything. He could have put his fist through the hole he now felt. Blood drenched his hand.

"You haven't got long, friend," said Gunn. "You're breathing on one lung."

A bubble of blood appeared between the man's lips.

"Took my gold."

"You know them?"

"Moli . . ." he gasped.

"Don't try to talk. You say prayers?"

"Why?" Freddie Waite's eyes clouded over, misted with a milky film.

"Might be a good time to make peace with your maker."

"I got a clear conscience."

Gunn looked at the man. In his late forties, thin enough to slip through a slat fence, light brown hair, hazel eyes, a half day's stubble on his chin. It was a tough time to die. A man ought to live out his years if he could. Waite wouldn't. He had done the work and somebody had come and taken it all away. This wasn't claim jumping. This was robbery—and murder.

Another spasm ripped through Waite's body.

Gunn started to say something when he heard hoofbeats. He lay Freddie down gently, stretched to reach his rifle.

15

Too late.

"Mister, you touch that rifle and I'll blow your brains from here to kingdom come."

Gunn looked up.

The voice was a woman's.

The shotgun in her hands was cocked.

Both triggers.

CHAPTER TWO

"Are you one of them?"

Gunn looked up at the woman on horseback and felt his scalp prickle. Her finger was inside the trigger guard of the sawed-off double-barreled shotgun. If she even twitched, he was a dead man.

"No," he said quietly.

"Back away slow," she said, her voice even as rain on water. Her eyes were as blue as columbines, as periwinkles. Blue as a deep mountain lake. Her hair was so black it had a sheen to it, bright as a crow's wing. Her skin was dusky, her face tanned from the sun. Her jaw was heart-shaped, firm; her cheekbones high, graceful. Gunn glimpsed all of this in a moment, but his mind was on that finger inside the trigger guard.

He sideslipped away from the wounded man, careful to avoid going near his rifle. The woman's gaze never wavered. Her lips, full and ripe, puckered in thought as her eyes followed him. He was grateful that her hands did not shake. The shotgun held steady.

"Pa?" she breathed. "Pa, did they hurt you bad?"

17

"He's hurt bad," said Gunn, his voice soft. "He's only got a few minutes."

"Shut up!" she exclaimed, a light flashing in her blue eyes.

"I didn't shoot him."

Freddie himself saved Gunn from being shot that moment. He groaned, tried to move. The woman's attention shifted to the wounded man, who was evidently her father.

"Lorelei . . ." he croaked.

"You, stay where you are," she said, flicking a glance at Gunn. "I'll be right there, Pa."

She dismounted, her jodhpurs whispering against the saddle, her riding boots thudding on the ground. She held the shotgun deftly, but now her finger was outside the trigger guard. Gunn breathed his first good breath, but held his place. She was young and quick and he didn't want to wind up as another of the mistakes that had been made here this day.

Freddie Waite coughed and Gunn saw blood bubbles appear at the corners of his mouth. Lorelei winced, lay down her shotgun. She leaned over her father, ignoring Gunn.

"Pa, don't die, please."

"This man . . . helped me."

"Yes," she said, tears filling her eyes. "Let me help you. Does it hurt very bad?"

"It doesn't hurt . . . at all."

Gunn let out a breath. When it didn't hurt anymore, that was a sign of the end. He had seen it happen before—with a man, an animal. A kind of peace settled over those creatures who were dying. A mercy that he couldn't explain. He had felt the same thing when he

18

had come close to death. Some kind of dullness of feeling, of the spirit, a laziness crept through a man's senses at such times so that death didn't matter. Nothing mattered.

"Miss," said Gunn, "we'd best get him out of the sun."

She turned to him, her cheeks wet with tears.

"Yes."

And the same numbness gripped her, he saw. He stood up, walked over to Freddie Waite. He knelt down, shoved his arms under the man's back and legs. He lifted him up, surprised at his lightness. Lorelei ran ahead, to the cabin. She stumbled up the steps, opened the door. Gunn carried the wounded miner inside. It was cool in the front room.

"Where?" he ventured.

"In his room," she said, her voice weak, no longer like rain on water, but like the sound of dust blowing across desert flowers. Her voice was all muffled and distant as if it did not belong to her at all.

He followed her through a doorway into a bedroom. A man's room. The room of a man who did not need much but a soft bed after a hard day's work. A chair, a picture on the wall, a table where he could sit and smoke, a chest of drawers where he could keep his things, a wardrobe for his few clothes.

Lorelei smoothed the bed, fluffed a pillow.

Gunn laid her father atop the coverlet, slipped his arms free. His left hand was wet with fresh blood. He tried to hide it from Lorelei.

"I'll leave you two alone," he said, walking backwards.

She seemed not to hear him, but draped her body

over the bed, began caressing her father's forehead. She touched him as if he were made of glass, as if afraid he would break if she touched him too hard. He watched the two for a moment and then turned to walk through the cabin. Somewhere, there might be water. He was thirsty and his eyes still stung from the wind-blown grit that had stabbed at them for better than forty miles.

The kitchen was big enough. There was water in buckets and in a pitcher. The wood stove was small, not the best. It would rust out in another year. The table was rustic. There were only two chairs. Everything was neatly hung and put away. The floor was swept, the counters clean. He drank the water out of the pitcher and felt it slide against the raw wound of his throat. He gasped for air and knew he would be sick if he drank more. He wanted more. He refilled the pitcher, found a glass in the cupboard. He carried them back to the front bedroom. There was another bedroom beyond the kitchen, but he had not looked into it. The door was opened only a few inches. Lorelei's room, he figured.

She was holding her father's face in her hands, though her head was buried in the pillow next to him. Her body shook as if she was sobbing, but Gunn heard no sound. He set the pitcher and the glass on the dresser, trying not to make any noise.

He started to walk out of the room.

"What is your name?"

He turned, saw that she had raised up, was looking at him.

"Gunn."

"Just Gunn?"

"That's all."

"He's dying, isn't he?"

20

"Yes. You can't stop the bleeding. I'm sorry."

"I—I felt his back. It just keeps coming out."

"It's slower than some I've seen, ma'am. Not an artery. Just a bunch of veins. But a bunch of them."

"God, I feel so helpless."

"Just give him all you have while he's here." Gunn's eyes clouded so that they appeared to be paler than robin's eggs. He left the room, even though she was still talking to him.

"Come back in a while," she said. "Don't go away yet."

"No. I've got a horse up on the hill." He stopped, looked back through the doorway.

"I've a pack mule. Would you bring it up? I'd be obliged."

"Yes'm."

Gunn was glad to get away. He was a coward at such times. What could he say to a daughter whose father was dying? Dying in the worst possible way. There would be more to his death than just the bleeding and the bad breathing. Death was ugly at times. Violent death was uglier than any other. Gunn knew.

Esquire was frantic for water. Gunn took him to the stock tank, left him hitched while he sought out the pack mule Lorelei had left on its own. He found the animal on the side of the road, the knot in its rope caught between two rocks. He led the animal back to the cabin, noticing, for the first time, the sign that read, "LUCKY GIRL MINE," painted on a board that was nailed to a stake just outside the cave.

He led his horse and the mule to the corral, stripped them and set out fodder he found in a bin. He lugged his saddle to a rustic tack room, set it and the bridle, blankets and rifle scabbard inside. He picked up his rifle and lugged his saddlebags to the cabin. He went back for the goods he had taken off the mule's back, sacks of cans, flour, whatnots. He carried those inside, set them in the kitchen. He left his gear on the porch, drank more water, and rolled a cigarette in the front room.

Not much there, either. Some faded flowers on tables, a stone fireplace, a narrow mantel. Knick-knacks on that. A divan, a couple of chairs stuffed with ticking, some bare wooden ones that were stacked with old newspapers, magazines. The windows had shutters and these were cut with rifle holes. People lived here, but they lived with constant wariness. There were boxes of ammunition near each window, and an old Henry .44-.40 with octagonal barrel leaning in a corner. A pistol was shoved under the newspapers, its butt protruding. It was not a good way to live and Gunn wondered, again, if it was worth it to try to own something that other men envied or sought. He had lived that way once, and had lost the most precious thing in his life—his wife. And now he did not own anything but what he had on his back and on his horse. He had money, but he carried very little with him. In not owning anything, he had come to realize something that he had never known before. He owned everything. Wherever he camped, that was his land, and sometimes it stretched beyond where his eyes could reach. Wherever he lived for a time, that was his possession. He owned mountains and rivers and creeks and timber and game, but it cost him nothing. He paid no taxes and he had no salaries to make out each month. He had the sky and the earth and that was more than most men had if they chose to live in cities and buy property that they had to defend and work for like slaves.

He built a cigarette, lit it. The cabin was quiet, yet it seemed to breathe. The windmill had stopped churning for a moment. He no longer heard its screech. He thought about the man in the next room. The man was dying and his daughter could only look on helplessly. He wondered that a man would bring his daughter to a place like this. It was desolate, hot, isolated. No place for a young woman. She had been to a town, brought back supplies. But what kind of a town did they have out here? A mining town. The worst kind.

He sucked the smoke in, held it.

His thirst came back, but he could handle it now that he knew there was water. Not having it had made it precious. Was that what craving was? Wanting something you knew you couldn't have?

"Mister Gunn?"

Her voice startled him. He was lost in thought, the cigarette burning to ash in his hand.

He turned around, saw her standing there, holding on to the doorjamb.

"Yeah?"

"My pa—he's real bad. His—his color . . ."

"I'll be right there." Gunn stood up, snubbed out his cigarette in a clay *cenicero*. The windmill started up again, its screech like a wounded animal, like some keening beast in the flames of hell.

Lorelei sat next to the bed, dabbing her father's forehead with a damp cloth. A column of sunlight slanted through the windows, motes of dust danced golden in the shimmering shaft of seemingly motionless light.

23

Freddie Waite wheezed with a single lung. His lips were blue as if he had been nibbling on berries. His cheeks were sunk, his face drenched with sweat.

Gunn walked to the opposite side of the bed.

He put two fingers to the dying man's jugular. Felt the erratic pulsing of the man's blood. The pulse was not steady. It was lumpy, as though the man's blood was made of beads and thread. The thread was thinning out and the beads were getting smaller.

"Can you do anything?" asked Lorelei.

Gunn leaned over, rubbed the man's chest over the heart. He didn't know if it would do any good, but he had seen a sawbones do it once to a man in shock from loss of blood.

Freddie's eyes opened. He drew a fair breath and did not cough.

"I'll cash in soon," he whispered. "Lorelei, it don't hurt none."

"Pa, I—I love you. Can't you hold on?"

"I want to. Tell him about them."

Lorelei's eyes misted. She nodded.

Gunn stopped massaging the man's chest. There was pain there. Somewhere. The man didn't want to die. That was pain enough. He struggled for breath. Sometimes he could get air and sometimes it would not come back out. If it came out, it was hard to draw back in. Ragged. Like the way water sucked in and out of a sinkhole at low ebb. Godawful to hear, to see.

"Six bags of dust they stole," said Freddie, his voice barely audible.

"Pa, it's not important."

"They'll file on the claim now."

Gunn and Lorelei exchanged looks. His eyebrows

arched. His lean, tanned face took on a copper-gold hue in the column of sunlight pouring through the window. Lorelei's eyelashes dipped like diminutive flags as she held tightly to her father's hand.

"Don't worry about it," said Gunn. "If you filed . . ."

"Listen," Freddie rasped, "they'll do her. You got to watch out for Snake and Chigger. Not them, but . . ."

Lorelei's face chalked. Her father's breath faltered, got caught in his chest. His complexion turned blue. She leaned over her father. Gunn, alarmed, brushed her aside. His hand grazed against one of her breasts. She glared at him with flashing eyes for a moment.

Gunn bent down, pushed against Freddie's chest. He grabbed the dying man's mouth, put his mouth to Freddie's and forced his breath into his lungs. Waite gasped, choked. His breath caught, became thready, settled into an even pace again.

"Thanks," said Waite, after a few moments. "I reckon it won't be long. That last one made me ice up all over. Felt like I was electrified."

"Save your breath," said Gunn.

"No. You got to promise me something. Lorelei's all alone now. You got to clear my claim. She knows I filed. Ain't official yet, but I damn sure filed."

Gunn looked at Lorelei. Her face hardened into a frozen mask. The fear she felt inside rushed to the surface, glassed over her eyes. Her skin turned waxen; her lips tightened into a frown.

"Mister, I'm about to run out of road. Can you make me that promise?"

Lorelei's eyes never flickered.

Gunn drew in a breath.

"You got my promise," he said.

Freddie tried to smile. Instead, an involuntary shudder twisted his mouth into a grimace. His eyes closed. This time, the spasm did not pass. Freddie died with a rattle in his throat that sounded like pebbles in an empty tin can. His left hand twitched in Lorelei's, and then was still.

Gunn looked at her.

She stared at her father with vacant eyes.

Tears flowed silently down her cheeks.

"It looks like he ran out of road," said Gunn.

"He—he's dead?" She looked up at him, eyes wide, eyebrows arched in puzzlement.

Gunn nodded.

Lorelei threw herself on her father as if to give him life.

Gunn walked away, leaving her alone with her grief. Damn the man. He hadn't died soon enough. Now, Gunn had made a promise. A promise to a dead man.

A promise he would honor.

CHAPTER THREE

Gunn buried Frederick Waite in the cool of morning.

Lorelei shivered in the chill, read the psalm about the valley of the shadow of death.

When she closed the Bible, the sound echoed through the cave, the candle on the ledge flickered.

She looked at Gunn, her eyes no longer misted. Instead, there was anger there, hard and cold as blue agates.

"Come inside the cabin," she said. "I have coffee brewed. You can be on your way before the sun's high."

"I made your pa a promise."

"I won't hold you to that. It was a deathbed promise. Made his going the easier for him."

She walked toward the mine entrance, toward the pale gray light at the end of the shaft. Gunn looked at the pile of stones that marked Waite's grave, reached up and snatched the candle from the ledge. The flame flickered out. For a moment, as Lorelei passed through the opening, it was dark inside the cave, the tomb.

He did not go inside the cabin for a time. Instead, he saw to the horses and mules. The windmill was silent, but there was water in the troughs. It had gotten chilly during the night but there was no frost. He gave Esquire a handful of extra grain, rubbed his coat with a scrap of saddle blanket. He built a smoke and saw the morning take shape as the sun boiled over the horizon, a giant red globe in the far haze.

Lorelei was packing saddlebags with food when he finally entered the cabin. There was hardtack and cooked bacon, cans of beans and peaches. She looked up when he came in the back door, her eyes still hard with anger.

"Coffee'll be bitter if you don't have some soon."

The aroma filled the kitchen. The heat from the stove was welcome after the chill of morning, the dankness of the cave.

"I'll have a cup. You going somewhere?"

"I am."

She closed the flap on a saddlebag, took down cups from the cupboard, set them on the table. Gunn watched her as she deftly handled the hot coffeepot, poured the steaming brew. She used her skirt to keep her hand from being burnt by the handle. He saw a flash of petticoat, ankle. The contrast against the black of her dress was startling. But Lorelei herself was startling. She sat down at the table, lifted her cup, blew on it.

"Thank you for taking care of the stock," she said evenly. "My mind wasn't on it this morning."

Gunn shrugged. The coffee was too hot to drink, even after blowing on it. He itched to build a smoke. He was not hungry. The bacon smell still clung to the room. He was stiff from sleeping on the floor, but it beat hard ground.

"I meant it about the promise," she said.

"So did I, when I made it."

"No. You wanted to ride on. You still do. You're a drifter, a saddletramp."

Her words stung, but he said nothing. His shirt, open at the collar, was sweaty from the burial; his clothes smelled of horse and greasewood.

"Am I right?"

She wasn't sure.

"I reckon," he said quietly, the trace of a smile flickering on his lips.

Gunn was a shade over six feet, with not an ounce of fat on him. His wide shoulders set square on his torso. His pale gray-blue eyes bespoke wisdom and depth and she searched those out, now, perhaps wondering if that was all that he was—a drifter.

"I wanted you last night. Bad."

Gunn almost choked on his swallow of coffee.

"You're shocked?"

"Surprised," he said.

"I want you now. Before you go."

"You don't know me."

"It was the same when Ma died. When my brother died. A lonely feeling, a feeling of being mortal. At first I thought it was just me and that it was wrong to want a man when a loved one died."

"What changed your mind?"

"Pa, and some other people. When my ma was killed, we thought we were all going to die. The Apache Indians attacked us one afternoon. We were all at a party near a valley called Mesilla. I was ten years old.

29

The Indians rode through, shooting and screaming. Then they were gone. Ma was dead and some of the men. Pa went to sleep that night with my aunt, my mother's sister. And the other women took men to bed with them. Later, I asked my aunt about all this."

"And what did she tell you?"

"She said when you lost a loved one, that was when you most wanted to be touched, to be embraced, to be kissed."

"To make love."

"You know?"

"Yes," said Gunn, standing up. "I know."

Lorelei rose from the table, went to him.

"Hold me," she said simply.

Gunn put his arms around her. He felt her heart beating. Her breasts were soft. They flattened against his chest and he felt the warmth from her thighs. Her black dress crinkled and made a rustling sound. She put her arms around him and squeezed him tight. He felt her body trembling.

Yes, he knew how it was. When Laurie died. He thought it was unnatural to even think about lying with another woman, but since then he had learned that people wanted love at the oddest times. He had seen men and women couple when they were in grave peril. He had seen dying men cry out for a woman. He had seen widows couple with strangers just after seeing their husbands die brutally. He thought that it was probably a survival thing: Nature's way of preserving the species. Yet he had seen no animal in the wilds behave so. Only people. And he had come to accept this as a part of life.

"I still want you," she crooned. "More than ever."

"Is it death? Does death scare you?"

"I don't know. Maybe. I just feel godawful lonesome."

She tilted her head up and he bent to kiss her. Her lips were pliant, yielding. He kissed her gently, then felt the fire in her. Her body surged against his and her trembling went away.

He knew about the lonesome.

Sometimes it got so bad he thought about things he shouldn't think about. The last miles on the desert were such that he had wondered if he would ever come to the end of it. He could deal with the days, with the sun, the heat, but when the nights closed in on him and the trail was empty and long, he would miss his woman and the friends he once had. He carried no bitterness with him. He had chosen his own path and he blamed no one for that. The emptiness, the loneliness was a thing not of his choosing. It came unbidden and he lived through it. He recognized it in others. He saw its enormity, now, in Lorelei, felt it in her touch, her quivering body against his.

"Come," he said, "I will take you to bed. We will lie there and think about these things."

"Gunn, you make me tremble all over."

"You can't see what's happening to me. It is the same."

"You appear very calm, very sure of yourself."

"I am sure of myself, but a man is never sure of a woman."

She touched his face with a single cautious hand. Her finger tips touched his high cheekbones, the flat of his nose, traced a gentle path across his lips and chucked his strong chin. Her eyes gazed into his, probing, questioning. She drew in a deep breath. He cracked a lazy smile.

"You have stirred me," he said, "and I can walk away right now, even so. But if you keep looking at me with those blue eyes, I will either melt or turn savage. I have ridden a long way and I have seen no women across the desert."

"My God," she panted, "the way you talk, the husk in your voice. You make me burn up inside. I—I wanted you before, but only because you were here and I was here. Now, I . . . I . . . ache for you, Gunn."

The twitch in his groin made him grip her shoulders with firm hands.

Her eyes worked their magic on his senses.

"Take me to your bed, then," he said gruffly.

She plucked at him with desperate fingers, then grabbed his arm, led him from the kitchen. A lizard on the sill above the door twitched its tail, blinked as they passed by. Its throat throbbed with a breathy pulse; its mouth hung open as if it had been saved from drowning.

He followed her like a man drugged on opium.

A door opened. Gunn saw her disappear, hurried to catch up. She was waiting for him.

"Hold me tight," she whispered. "Just hold me tight as you can."

She smelled of crushed desert flowers and strong soap. She smelled of female powders and the mysterious musk a woman gives off when she wants love. She nuzzled against his chest and he buried his face in her clean, dark hair.

Gunn wanted her.

His pants' crotch stretched taut.

A man oughtn't to want a woman in the harsh unfair light of day like that, Gunn thought, but he couldn't remember when he wanted anyone more. Maybe it was because of the way she so boldly approached him. Maybe it was the way he felt when he held her in his arms. Maybe it was only because she was a woman and he a man.

Her room was as modest as a slave's crib, yet he saw that she had brightened it with dried flowers, cactus plants in earthen pots, swatches of woven cloth dyed vivid colors tacked to the walls. The bed was home-made, as was the rest of the furniture: a table, chair, wardrobe. Light spilled through the two windows. There was no mirror in the room, but a basin and pitcher of water sat on a long box that had been sanded and varnished. The bed was barely big enough for two people, had been built against the wall in one corner. Lorelei broke the embrace, turned down the thin comforter that served as a bedspread. She seemed suddenly self-conscious.

"I've never had a man come to my room before."

She was not apologizing, he knew. She seemed proud. Either proud that she had been chaste while her father was alive or proud that Gunn was to be the first.

"No'm," he said, suddenly uncomfortable. He hesitated. She rushed to him, took his arm.

"Don't leave," she said. "I couldn't bear that. Not after I've come this far, shamed myself so much. It's just that . . . this has been my sanctuary, the place I always came when life got too hard to bear. My pa respected my privacy."

"You've had no suitors come to call?"

She laughed harshly, released her grip on his arm.

33

"No man would ride this far for a woman," she said. "They go to San Diego or to Los Angeles, or to the big ranchos along the seacoasts. They do not ride out here to the edge of the desert."

There was no bitterness in her tone. She appeared to have accepted her fate, harsh as it was.

"I would ride this far," he said.

She looked at him intently, as if trying to fathom meaning in his smoky eyes.

"I *have* come this far." Gunn began to unbutton his shirt.

Lorelei dipped her lashes modestly, then began to mimic his movements. Her fingers worked at the fastenings of her black mourning dress.

CHAPTER FOUR

Her skin was dark where the sun and the wind had scorched her, white as lilies where her clothes had kept her covered. Her arms and hands were brown, so was her neck and face. She had freckles on her shoulders, above her breasts. Her breasts were white except for the dark aureoles, the flattened, tucked-in nipples. The black thatch between her legs contrasted sharply with the alabaster complexion of her thighs.

She stood there, waiting for him to come to her.

Gunn wanted her very much.

The sun rose in the sky and the room took on a golden cast. Motes of dust danced in the thin shafts of light that slanted through the shuttered windows. The windmill began its mournful, screeching song as cool air rose from the earth, met the warming currents above the land.

"Am I pleasing to you?" she asked.

"Yes," he replied, huskily.

"You think me shameless."

She did not move or try to hide her nakedness. She

did not fold her hands over her dark thatch, or cross her legs. She stood there, looking as pretty as any woman he had ever seen. As pure as anything he could ever want.

"No, I do not think that what a man and woman do with each other carries any shame. There is nothing shameful about your body or wanting a man to touch you."

"No matter what?"

"If they do not hurt others, no."

"You're a very unusual man."

Gunn felt the intensity of her glance. He was not yet hard, but he wanted her. Although it did not show in his bearing, he was churning inside. His stomach fluttered with a half-sick feeling. Desire clawed at his groin. He thought she was beautiful. More than that, he thought she was a very special woman. She acted neither coyly nor shamelessly. Rather, she seemed open and honest. She showed good breeding, even naked, a mien that few women possessed. She seemed to be a woman of quality, possessed of a nature he had seldom seen. He thought that such a woman might be very easy to fall in love with, that such a woman might make a man very happy over a long period of time. She was headstrong and purposeful. No doubt she had been very helpful to her father. Not many women of her age and comportment would stay in such a savage land without whimpering and whining. He detected none of this in her. She seemed to be a woman who had stuck through hard times and was willing to go on even after her father's brutal death. He admired her for that. He admired her for being honest about her womanly feelings.

"You're very beautiful," he said. "I want you, if you still want me."

"Yes. Hold me. Kiss me first."

His heart wrenched in his chest to hear her words. He strode to her, took her in his arms. It was better this way. Without the black, shining dress, without the look of mourning in her eyes. Her flesh against his was a tingling, warming sensation. Her breasts pressed into his chest and the hardness that was not there came instantly when she urged her loins into his.

He kissed her.

He was not prepared for the savagery of her response. Her mouth opened and he breathed the steam of her heat. Her body leaped against his, the bristly thatch between her legs scratching his groin with a sensuous, spidery touch.

He slid his tongue between her lips, into her mouth. She opened it wider and he felt her tongue delve into his own mouth. She moved her hands on his arms, plucking the hard muscles, kneading the tendons with eager fingers.

She sucked away his breath. Her warm body seemed to grow into his own. His cock hardened into a throbbing mass of swollen, blood-engorged veins. They kissed until they were breathless with passion. They clung to each other like people drowning.

"I—I can't wait any more," she gasped.

"Let me take you to bed, Lorelei."

"Yes, yes. Take me to bed. Take me here. Now. I can feel you. I want you inside me so bad my legs are weak."

He led her to the bed, in a trance. He touched her buttocks, rubbed them, wanting her. He reached out for her, drew her against him. His swollen cock slid underneath her buttocks, nestled against her cleft. He fought to keep from taking her then, without bed or pallet, from behind, like an animal. She pressed her buttocks against him, raising them so that he could easily have slipped into her. The urge in him was strong, as strong as it had ever been for any woman.

He pushed her away from him, onto the bed. She did not turn over, but waited there, her buttocks high, her sex-cleft, furred over with pubic hairs, presenting itself in a most appealing manner. He climbed up behind her, mounted her. He slid into her sheath. His mind was gone. It was in his loins, in his pulsing shaft that seeped clear fluids hot as broth.

"Oooh," she moaned, thrusting backwards.

He sank deep, straddling her legs and buttocks. His hands grasped her breasts, held them gently while he humped her. She shuddered, climaxed. He slid out, as she pitched forward.

She turned over, spread her legs.

"I want to see you first," she said.

He looked at her pubic thatch once again. There was the secret, the mystery. There was the woman waiting. There was the only place where he could be a part of her, where she could be a part of him.

He lay beside her and she touched him. She was still trembling from the climax of seconds ago. She touched the hard rod that sprouted from his loins. It was slick with their juices. She squeezed him and he very nearly ejaculated. He sucked in a breath, fought against the overwhelming desire that flooded his loins.

"Lorelei," he said, "do you know what you are doing to me?"

"No," she admitted, "but I want to know everything

38

about you, your body, before you ride off and forget me."

Her words, as if they had form and body, lashed at him, stung his heart, made his stomach sink. She knew. And he loved her for knowing. Not many women would admit such a thing to themselves.

"It would be hard to leave you, Lorelei."

"But you will."

"I don't know."

"If we stopped now and didn't go any farther, would you stay longer?"

"Damnit, don't tease me, womaaan. I can't promise anything but to give you what I have right now."

"Only that?"

"That's all I have."

She opened her arms, rose up to him, her body willing and supple. He took her in his arms, crawled on top of her until his weight pressed her into the mattress on the bed.

"You have so much," she breathed. "You have everything I want and need right now."

Gunn looked into her blue eyes and smiled.

Lorelei's hunger was a deep and awesome thing to see, to feel. Gunn recognized it and felt it. Her yearning was as strong as his at that moment. He took her gently, mounting her as she plucked at his arms and shoulders with desperate fingers.

He sank to her naked body, probing the thick mat of dark hair at her cleft. She grasped his rock-hard cock and pulled it to her, arching her back to thrust her sex upward. A ripple of excitement made her body quiver wherever it touched his flesh.

He thrust downward, inward, probing. The mushroom crown of his penis pushed against the soft lips of her cunny. She gasped with pleasure as he slid past the plush labia. She was wet, her tunnel oiled with the ooze of desire.

"Yes, Gunn, yes," she breathed.

He sank his shaft into the steaming sheath of her sex. She bucked with a sudden spasm. Blood throbbed in his temples with a muffled thunder. Lorelei cooed pleasure as he filled her with himself. He stroked her, held her tight as he kissed her wet lips, tongued her mouth.

Her second orgasm came suddenly. She thrashed like a colt cinched up for the first time under a saddle. He rode her through the awesome shudders until her body turned pliant as a willow shoot. Her thigh muscles spasmed, twitched, until he felt the squeezing of his shaft. The pleasure was electric, exquisite.

Her hands rubbed his shoulders, his arms. He settled into a smooth rhythm of strokings, plumbing the deepest recesses of her smolder-warm cavity. There, deep inside her, it was all volcanic heat and molten flow, the warmth soaking into him, stirring his pouched seed until it threatened to boil and explode. He arched his back, bent to her breasts. He kissed them, teasing the nipples to hard nubbins with his tongue. Her loins slammed into his as another orgasm jolted her, shuddered through her flesh like a wind that rushes over the mountains without warning and rustles the prairie grasses. Like a wind that rattles through an empty cornfield when the dead husks and the skeletal stalks are dry.

The morning sun streamed through the shuttered windows, warming the room. Gunn stroked her fast now and his sleek body glistened with the sweat of his passion. Lorelei, too, became oiled with sweat, the dampness flattening her hairline.

She wrapped her legs around his hips and they rocked together in perfect tempo until she spasmed again. This time, the orgasm stretched out into a timeless chain and her eyes closed with the pleasure of it. She did not stop her rhythmic bucks as the sensation suffused her body, took control of her.

"I want you to come," she said.

Gunn needed no urging. Her writhing body seemed to pull him deeper inside her. He gorged himself on her beauty, sated himself on her warmth, the deep wetness of her sex-cavern. She kissed him demandingly, pulled at him until he felt his seed burst from its sac.

"Oh, yes, I feel it," she said, thinking that she did. Rather, she felt his shuddering body, the quick jabs of his manhood spurting the milky sperm. She raked his back with clawing fingers, bucked a final time with a convulsive orgasm.

He died inside her. Died the good death of pleasure.

She moaned softly, stroked his damp hair away from his forehead. She looked into his eyes, scanned his face. Her eyes were shining with the radiance of a woman well-loved, satisfied. He lay atop her, a half smile on his lips, full of her still.

"You linger," she said quietly. "Most men would be . . ."

"How do you know?"

"Some men."

He didn't ask her more. He did not want to know about the other men. To him, she seemed special, his own woman. Like the first woman. Like Laurie, his

41

wife. She glowed. Her warm body comforted him, though his manhood was sapped, without energy, force.

"You're a fine woman," he said.

"Thank you for that."

"I mean it, Lorelei."

"You say that now, but you'll ride off and I'll never see you again."

"I made a promise."

"Yes, men make promises. To get something. To take something."

His eyes went cloudy.

"I—I'm sorry," she said. "I didn't mean to be cruel."

He squeezed her a last time, rolled to her side. He did not move away, but put a hand on her leg. He stared at the ceiling, felt the heat of the room rise up. It was going to be another sweltering day.

"Unpack your saddlebags," he said. "We need this day to ourselves. The men who took the gold will not hurry."

"What?"

"I want to grease that damned windmill, spend a night with you."

"But, those men . . . they'll file on the mine."

Gunn lifted himself up, looked down at her.

"Tell me about the mine. Did your father file on it or not?"

Lorelei frowned. She rubbed a finger down her sweat-sleek tummy. Gunn wanted her again.

"Freddie filed a claim in his name. He was—was going to make it a joint ownership, put my name on it, but he never got around to it."

"So?"

"He left no will."

"Damn."

"There's another thing."

"Tell me," he said.

"When Freddie—Pa—filed, it was another piece of property. Right next to this one. He kept working the side of the mountain, not paying any attention to much else. Then he struck a vein. He blasted, followed it on through."

"But he didn't file on the new claim."

"He meant to. Any day now. But the vein was so rich, he just kept going and we never did file a new claim."

Gunn whistled.

"Anyone else know about this?"

"Maybe. I'm not sure."

"But he staked it."

"Yes."

"Maybe you're better off. If you have the measurements, you can file on it yourself."

"We never got around to that, either." Lorelei avoided Gunn's look. He got up from the bed, searched through his shirt for the makings. He built a cigarette, lit it. The aroma of tobacco filled the room. The bed creaked as Lorelei got up, sat on the edge.

"You must think I'm pretty dumb," she said.

"No. I just wonder if anyone bothered to check the old claim and come out here, run a survey."

"I—I don't think so. Pa had trouble with those two before, but they're just thieves."

"Yet you were worried about the old claim."

"Pa was. Maybe because of the new claim. I—I don't

know. I'm so mixed up."

"But you want to go after the two men who killed your father. Why?"

She looked up at him with steady eyes, blue as a high mountain lake and just as cold.

"I'm going to kill them," she said.

CHAPTER FIVE

Gunn greased the gears of the windmill, smearing thick petroleum over all the moving parts. He had found a bucket of grease among the mining tools in a small shack in back of the cabin. He had to pry the lid off with a hatchet blade. It was hot and he wore no shirt, a bandanna tied around his forehead to soak up the sweat. Lorelei was in the cabin, searching through her father's papers for the original claim.

The windmill was handmade, a pretty good job. The blades had been froed from strong cedar. They were light and wide, so to catch the wind. The grease helped. The windmill turned more easily in the air and didn't make as much noise. The gears were carved out of oak, didn't fit well. But they worked. Leather straps ran on wooden pulleys. These, too, he greased, until his arms and chest were smeared with it.

Water was precious and Gunn looked at the property with admiration. Freddie had built a small cistern up on the top of the rock wall and a drain ran to the house. There were wooden gutters around the roof and these, too, collected rain water, drained them into a pitch-tarred barrel in the kitchen. The man appeared obsessed with water and Gunn could understand why. If he had spent any time at all on the desert, prospecting, he would have a healthy respect for what a lot of folks took for granted.

When he had finished, Gunn took a walk around the property. He found two of the original claim stakes easily enough. The other two would be on a direct line, but which way? Freddie had probably staked out a good chunk, maybe twenty acres. Neither stake he found covered the mine blasted out of the hillside. He had been about ten feet short. But there were fresh stakes driven into the ground covering that mine too. These were behind the mountain. Smart. He walked through scrub pines, cedar, saw juniper growing on the slopes. Freddie had hacked his way down the slope behind the bowl canyon where his cabin was, figuring the vein went that way.

Gunn found diggings, test holes, all along the rock. Most were within the stakes, but some were far afield. Atop the cliff, he realized that he should never have found this place. It was not on the main road. Chance had brought him here, or instinct. He tried to think back, determine when he had left the trail across the desert. Esquire was partly responsible. He smelled water and they had headed for the nearest hills. Now, he saw that there were other trails, roads, a maze of them, just below the cabin. The men who had robbed and killed Freddie had taken one of them, heading west.

Waite's place was not in a good spot for defense. He was in a box and there were several directions in which men could ride in or ride out, taking advantage of cover. They could split up on several trails and a lone man would have trouble tracking them. Waite never had a chance. The thieves had waited until they had seen Lorelei leave, then come in, knowing they had Waite in a box from which there was no escape. They could have smoked him out or starved him out. But Waite had made it easy on them. He had fought for what he owned, what he had gouged out of the mountain with his bare hands.

Gunn found the other two stakes beyond the road facing the cabin. Again, for the new mine. Each one was shaved off on one side with the legend, "LUCKY GIRL MINE" carved into the wood. What then, Gunn wondered, was the first mine called?

He returned to the cabin. The sun was high in the sky. He picked up his shirt off the corral post, slung it over his shoulder.

Inside, Lorelei rushed to greet him. She threw her arms around him, kissed him fervently on the lips and face.

"I'm so happy we didn't leave right away," she said. "I've been thinking about how wonderful it was this morning."

She had a sheaf of papers in her hand.

"Look," she exclaimed. "Here are the measurements, the claim papers. Marked, 'Filed.'"

Gunn sat at the kitchen table. Lorelei leaned over his shoulders, resting her arms on his back. It felt good, intimate. She was like a young girl, happy, carefree.

Freddie had filed a claim all right. On the Lucky Girl Mine. But which was which? It might take a surveyor to get it straight. The date of filing was two years ago.

"And your pa hadn't filed on the new mine?"

"No. It's bad, isn't it?"

"I don't know. I found some stakes. The new mine is staked out proper. That should be good enough. But some papers would help. We'll take these, see what we can find out. Do you have any money?"

"Yes. In a San Diego bank and I've dust."

"We'll leave in the morning."

"I wouldn't care about the claim if you'd stay."

Gunn turned, stood up. His arms brushed the papers to the floor. He took her in his arms, kissed her. Lorelei returned his kiss eagerly.

"Would you forget about the men who killed your father?"

"No!" her eyes blazed. Gunn stepped back, facing a tigress. He would hate to cross such a woman. Her temper flared quick and there was a determined cast to her eye.

"Well, looks as though we have two things to do. Find the men who stole your dust and killed your pa, and file a new claim. Better find some measuring tape. We got a heap to do."

A smoky evening haze settled over the hills and the few thin clouds to the west hung there like strips of pink cloth, a soft rose by the setting sun. The coolness came in from the sea, pushed back the hot desert air. Gunn stood by the porch, riffling through the papers in his hand. He had slipped back into his shirt after watering the stock, washing up at the corral. He felt better than he had in days. Lorelei was a part of it, but so was being in the hills after days crossing dry hostile land clear

48

from the Colorado at Yuma.

He had measurements, dozens of them. It had been a long, hot afternoon, but Freddie Waite may have known what he was doing after all. Gunn didn't know the mining laws, but the stakes were plain and by his calling the new mine the same as the old one, he just might be covered—legally.

Lorelei came out on the porch, smiled at him. She was freshly scrubbed, wore a small cluster of desert flowers in her hair. It was brushed to a high sheen, tied in back with a yellow ribbon.

"What do you think?" she asked, looking at the mass of papers in Gunn's hand.

"Don't know. Have to see a lawyer or someone at the claim office. I have a hunch, though."

"Do you believe in hunches?"

"If they work." He grinned.

"Well?"

"I think your pa shorted himself on his first claim. All depends on where those other two stakes are. I can't find them and I think he might have pulled them up. Or someone did. The papers give measurements, but unless I miss my guess, your pa played it loose."

"Sounds like him. He always liked to have an ace in the hole. He built a cistern, then dug a well. He kept waterbags in the mine where they would be cool."

"Smart man."

"Yes. Until this morning."

Gunn held out his hand. His heart beat rapidly whenever he was near her. She was a beautiful woman. Made more beautiful by loving than any he had ever known, except Laurie. He had seen her weeping privately a couple of times when she had been looking

49

at things her father had done. Yet she showed little of her grief. And none of it seemed to be self-pity. She missed her father, but she accepted the fact that he was gone.

She took his hand, came down the steps.

It was a good moment. She smelled good. She clasped his hand firmly, squeezed it. He felt a tingle of sensation up and down his spine. Gunn was in his late twenties. Lorelei was young, not yet twenty. He wondered, sometimes, if he would ever marry again. Would ever find the right woman. The ones he liked were all Laurie's age—the age she had been when he met her, or the age she had been when she died. Oh, he had met some women his own age, but they didn't possess the quality he sought, the special innocence Laurie had possessed. It was a quirk with him, he knew. Something he had seldom admitted to himself. He had only recognized it recently as time wore on, as he approached thirty.

"We missed the sunset," she said.

"I know."

"Pa and I used to walk up to the top of the cliff and watch it sometimes. He said it made him feel good."

"It does. So does a sunrise."

"Gunn, you're an odd man. I don't know much about you."

"There's not much to know."

"You're a drifter. But I think there's a reason for that."

"There's a reason. A reason for everything."

"You came here. You saw my father die."

"Yes."

"I've wondered about that all day. I saw you out

there. Fixing the windmill. Walking around. Taking care of the stock. Not many men would care enough to do those things."

He looked at her, wondered what point she was trying to make.

"You checked a lot of things."

"You spying on me?"

"Don't be funny. Yes. I was watching you because I saw a difference in you. I was curious."

"You curious about something in particular?"

She stood away from him, looked him up and down. He felt her scathing glance, tried a wry smile. It didn't work. Her expression grew serious. She did have a point to make. He knew that.

"You look like a man who can handle himself. You've got a good horse, a pistol. A Winchester rifle. Yet, you did nothing to save my father. You watched him being shot down and you never tried to help."

Gunn reached for her. She was cracking. Her voice quavered. She was on the verge of hysteria. Tears welled up in her eyes. She pushed him away. He felt the hurt like a stab in the heart. He reached out for her again, but she backed away, her eyes glittering with a savage light.

And in her hands was his Colt .45, snatched from his holster before he realized what she was doing.

She raised the Colt chest-high with both hands.

The hammer clicked as she drew it back with her thumb to full cock.

Her hands held steady.

Gunn broke out in a cold sweat.

There was a crazy glint in Lorelei's eyes. He froze, his hands suspended in midair. He could hear the seconds of his life ticking away in the silence.

Lorelei's finger slid inside the trigger guard.

"Hey, Lorelei," said Gunn, "that's a light trigger."

Her finger stiffened, stopped moving a scant half-inch from the trigger.

But that wild look was still cast in her eyes. She appeared to look past Gunn in a fixed stare. The effect on him was unnerving. He felt as if Lorelei was beyond reach of his voice, of reason. He had a compulsion to move a hand in front of her face to test her eyesight. Yet he did not move. Her finger was too close to the trigger. Her hand was too steady. At this short range, she couldn't miss—even with her eyes closed.

"Lorelei?"

Her eyes blinked and seemed to come back into focus.

"Lorelei?" he asked again.

"Don't you make a move, mister," she said, her voice oddly off-key. Again, that cast in her eye. The thousand-yard stare, the kind he had seen sometimes in the men he commanded during the war. In the boys' eyes when the mist was rising from the ground and bayonets were fixed. You knew the charge was coming, but not when. Confederates in the woods. Artillery pointed right at your throat. That kind of stare.

"I'm not moving," said Gunn calmly.

"You are one of them, aren't you?"

"Lorelei, no."

"You could have saved my pa. You had this pistol."

"I was too far away. Those boys had me pinned down."

"Excuses! Poor Freddie. He never had a chance. I should have been here. I'm a better shot."

"His rifle jammed," said Gunn.

"That old rifle? Yes, I told him about it. He kept it in the mine anyway. Said it was good enough for varmints, four-legged or two-legged."

Gunn measured the distance. As long as she kept talking, she'd be distracted. Even though the pistol did not waver, she was not concentrating on him. She stood like a statue, her voice sounding oddly mechanical.

"You can't bring him back, Lorelei. What happened, happened."

"Who are you, really?" she asked. "Are you wanted by the law? Are you after the claim too?"

It was now or never. Her finger had moved closer to the trigger. If she sneezed, the Colt would go off. The hammer had been on an empty cylinder. Now that it was cocked, the hammer would come down on a loaded cartridge. He'd have one hell of a chest pain that no poultice could cure.

Gunn dropped quickly to a squatting position and dove for Lorelei's legs.

Her finger squeezed the trigger.

The Colt boomed.

An orange flame blossomed from the barrel.

Lead whistled through the air and the dusk was shattered with the sound of the explosion.

CHAPTER SIX

Gunn slammed into Lorelei's waist, driving like a maddened bull.

The explosion cracked his eardrums, filled them with a high-pitched ringing. A rush of hot air suffocated him. Hot powder peppered his forehead, stung his flesh.

Lorelei flew backwards, knocked off balance by Gunn's rush, the impact of his body on hers. The pistol fell from her hands, hit the ground with a thud, the barrel smoking.

Gunn, deafened by the explosion, did not hear the air rush out of Lorelei's lungs as she landed hard on her back. She cushioned his own fall and he realized he had hit her hard. He raised up, looked down at her. She drew in a breath, blinked her eyes.

"Are you hurt?" he asked, slightly breathless.

A tiny fist smashed into his cheek. A foot came up, kicked him in the belly.

Lorelei screamed in rage.

She pelted him with fists, driving him away.

Gunn tried to grab her arms.

She clawed at him, her fingernails raking his cheek. He drew back in pain, his hand going to his face. Blood trickled down to his jawline. She snarled at him, hissed like some ferocious animal. Her hands flailed at him as he bobbed out of reach.

"Damnit, woman, come to your senses," he yelled gruffly.

She sat up, drew back a leg to kick him.

Gunn dove at the leg, grabbed it. He wrestled her back to the ground. Her dress slid up to her waist. Bare legs tried to clamp him in a vise grip. Lorelei, despite her youth and size, was strong. She was tough from hard work, resilient from years of surviving in a hostile land. She kicked, bit, scratched and pummeled him while he tried to smother her squirming body, get a grip on it. He didn't want to hurt her, but his reluctance was wearing him down. Her elbow slammed into his Adam's apple. He gasped for air. Lorelei followed up her advantage, shoving him hard against the corner of the porch.

He struggled to sit up.

Lorelei rammed her head into his midsection, knocking the air from his lungs. His throat hurt, burned like fire. He tried to say something, but the air just whistled through his mouth. She drove a first into his forehead and lights danced in his skull.

Then, as suddenly as it had begun, it was over.

Almost.

Lorelei stopped striking Gunn, even as he was wondering how to get her off his stomach. She sat, straddling him, staring down at his face, her fist cocked for another blow. Instead, she opened her hand, put

her arms around him, began kissing him. She slid down
onto his lap, began rubbing against his crotch. Her eyes
had not lost their wildness, but gleamed with a different
light.

Gunn didn't know what to make of it. But she was
rubbing him hard and he felt the pressure of her sex
pushing down into his groin.

"Oh, Gunn, I didn't mean it," she sobbed. "I'm
sorry."

Her mouth pressed against his, sucking at his lips,
her teeth nibbling him gently.

"Lorelei, what the hell . . ."

"Please don't get mad. I want you so bad, Gunn. I
can't stand it."

He had heard about such women, but had never met
one. Lorelei had changed from a savage, violent
woman to a purring kitten. His cock swelled with the
rubbing of her sex and desire flooded him. Her skirts
were hiked up to her hips and her bare legs were
tauntingly provocative. He wanted her bad and yet he
wondered how she could change so fast.

She tugged at his belt buckle, opened his trousers.
Her hands fished out his hardened penis. She rubbed
her crotch against his leg as she fondled him, staring at
his cock as if mesmerized.

Before he knew what was happening, Lorelei had
slipped off her panties, slid atop him, impaling herself on his penis. She raised and lowered herself on him
as she clutched his shoulders, staring at him with hard,
agate eyes. He found himself caught up madly in her
rhythm, matching it in counterpoint, smacking up into
her as she sank onto his cock.

She shuddered as orgasmic convulsions overtook her, again and again. Silently, she drove up and down, rising, falling, twisting, skewering her body with the swollen mass of flesh that rose from his crotch like an oversized scimitar. She varied her rhythms, undulated her hips, rotated them, touching every part of her love-sheath with his cock. She bent him to the limit, then brought him back before he cried out in pain. Her hair came loose, tumbled over her eyes, her shoulders. She hiked up her dress, stared down at the coupling, watched him slide in and out of her until her eyes closed and she shuddered with a private series of climaxes.

She moaned and uttered nonsense words, completely caught up in the act of sex itself. Gunn felt as if he was just an object to clear her mind of violent thoughts, an instrument like a doorknob, giving pleasure only because he was there, only because she needed him. It was an unnerving, fascinating experience. He watched her and felt as if he was watching a madwoman, a woman totally bereft of her senses. Her mouth fell open and her eyes closed as she rose up and down, pausing only when the spasms signified she was having still another climax.

He had no idea how long they lay like that as the sky darkened to gray, to purple and then to black. She rubbed him raw and then she went into a frenzy, bouncing up and down on him, his cock buried deep in her pussy, rocking back and forth, shouting at him insanely.

"Come, Gunn! Come, now!"

Gunn came.

With a sense of relief and release, he spewed out of

her, limp. His flesh tingled all over as if he had been massaged by a butcher. He stared up at her in the darkness, trying to see her eyes. He only saw her silhouette, faint. Her body was slick with sweat. She climbed off him, ruffled her skirt.

"I'll fix supper," she said softly, drifting away from him.

He heard her footfalls on the stairs. The door opening, closing. He lay in the dirt, totally stunned by his experience. He got up, tugged his trousers up snug, buckled his belt. He reached down, picked up something white. Lorelei's panties. They felt silken, sensuous.

He found his pistol, holstered it. It was dusty, with a spent shell in one of the cylinders. He would clean it later.

The stars winked on, first Venus, the evening star, then Mars, Jupiter. He drew a breath, looked at the glowing window in the cabin. Lorelei had lit a lamp in the front room. As if inviting him in. Gunn squeezed the panties in his hand. There was anger in him, and a deep sense of frustration.

Something inside him told him to run. To run, before it was too late. And then he thought about Lorelei and knew he could not run away. He had to find out more about her. He had to know what her innards were made of, what made her tick. He had to conquer her as she had conquered him, at least one more time.

The black widow scuttled down its web in the corner

of the kitchen. Its red hourglass marking glowed like an angry symbol. The spider leaped onto the trapped moth, sent shivering, lethal venom into its body. The moth was still. The spider began devouring its tail.

Gunn shook off the feeling of depression, tried to finish the food on his plate. Lorelei had not said ten words during supper. She sat there, her face pale and drawn, looking more like a woman grieving than at any time previously. Maybe her father's death had hit her, finally. He had seen such delayed reactions before. The food was good, a rich stew: beef, potatoes, onions, beans. Biscuits, honey from the Temecula hives, no butter. Tea. Yet Gunn was not hungry. Not for food. He kept looking at Lorelei, but she seemed lost in a world of her own.

She finished her dainty portions, scraped her chair getting up.

"I'm leaving before daybreak," she said.

"With me?"

"If you want to come along."

"Look, Lorelei . . ."

She cut him off.

"I think you'd best bunk in the front room tonight," she said.

"Fine." He resisted the urge to slam his fork into the plate. Instead, he set it down, rose from the table. "I'll get my bedroll."

"I've already put it out there," she said coldly.

He looked at her back as she stood at the sink. There was a lot of woman there. But something powerful bad was eating at her. She was cold, distant. There was a cruelty about the way she ignored him. He admitted to

59

the hurt it gave him to be so scorned. His stomach knotted up. A clammy feeling of total helplessness came over him.

He wanted to grab her shoulders, turn her around, kiss her hard on the mouth. He stepped close, saw her tense. No, this was not the time. Maybe it would never be the time. Whatever Lorelei had wanted from him, she had apparently gotten already.

"I'll see you in the morning," he said, his voice booming unexpectedly in the kitchen.

Lorelei didn't answer.

Gunn walked to the front room, laid out his bedroll. She had dumped it on the floor. He felt like a beggar, an interloper. Suddenly, the cabin got very small, suffocating. He wanted to leave, then. But he was tired, drained of energy. He had no wish to sleep on the trail. He walked outside, rolled a quirly. He lit it, smoked it slowly, trying to rein himself in.

No woman had ever gotten to him like Lorelei had. Not this deep. Yet he couldn't explain the attraction. Not anymore. So much had happened in one day that he found it hard to believe any of it had happened. She had seemed so warm and loving, and then she had turned cold, treating him like dirt. Was it grief, delayed to the point of anguish? Or had he stirred up some memories in her that she had buried a long time ago?

He finished the cigarette, ground it under his boot heel.

When he went back inside, the cabin was dark and still.

*   *   *

Sometime during the night, Lorelei came to him again, her hunger a raw and raging thing. She aroused him with her mouth and hands, savaged him with her body. Yet he gave in willingly. He gave her all he had, marveling at her strength, her energy. He took her on top, let her sit him as she would a horse. The sex was brutal, passionate, draining.

She mewed and purred, was alternately tender and lustful.

She growled and snarled, smacked her body against his with a terrifying abandon that made him once again question her sanity.

"Lorelei, why . . ."

"Don't, Gunn, don't ask me why. I need you. I need you so much I can't stand it."

That was all she said.

Before she left him, after the second time, she caressed him, running her fingers through his hair, touching his face. He felt a tenderness well up in him. Then, she did a remarkable thing. When he reached out to touch her, she grabbed his wrist, bit it hard. He cried out, jerked his wrist back. He was sure her teeth had struck bone.

"I'm sorry," she said, quickly. "I—I meant to kiss you, but I got carried away."

"You bite damned hard, lady," he snapped.

"I'd better go to bed. You should sleep."

Before he could say anything, she was gone. He held his wrist until the pain subsided. He could feel the teeth marks in the flesh. So far as he knew, there was no bleeding.

"Damn her," he muttered.

61

But he thought about her body, the way she made love. He wanted her so badly he almost got up and kicked her door down. Again, she was treating him like an intruder.

It was hell sleeping alone, knowing that in the next room there was a woman who made love like an Apache made war.

CHAPTER SEVEN

Esquire pranced friskly after Gunn stepped into the leather. He seemed as anxious to leave the bowl canyon as Gunn. The sky was just starting to pale in the east and both man and horse were bright, well-fed. Gunn waited for Lorelei to lead out, then gave Esquire his head. The horse switched his tail, stepped out briskly, following the black.

Gunn was surprised to find breakfast and coffee waiting for him when he climbed out of his bedroll. There was water heated for shaving and a fresh towel set out for him.

Lorelei was friendly, but carefully distant. She talked matter-of-factly about where they were going, what they were going to do. Only, now that he thought about it, she had never included him in her plans until that moment.

"That all right with you, Gunn?"

"I think we ought to find out who we're going up against," he said. "If this Snake and Chigger lit out of here for San Diego, they would have stopped somewhere. Next town."

"Julian. I imagine someone there knows them. We can stop at the Dry Gopher."

"Saloon?"

She nodded.

"Every drifter, bum, no-account goes in there. They'll probably talk to you. I'll meet you at the Julian Cafe when you're through."

Gunn nodded. At least Lorelei was cooperating.

"You have the papers we'll need?" he asked. He had left them on the table the night before.

"Yes," she said tightly.

She wore tight Californio trousers, a blouse, vest, a wide-brimmed sombrero. She carried a small-caliber pistol in a holster on her belt, another in a pouch she slung over her shoulder. She looked neat, self-assured. Her black hair was swept back, tied in a single braid that ran down her back. Her boots were polished, her spurs blunted, single-roweled. She saddled her own horse and carried a better rifle than the one her father had used when he was killed, a little Spencer carbine. Gunn had no doubt that she knew how to use every weapon she had on her. And meant to, if she ever came across the men who had killed Freddie.

The morning was cool and the sky overcast. With luck, they would not have the heat. Gunn was almost sure that the men who robbed and killed Waite would have laid over for a day. They had run their horses hard and themselves, as well. But even if they had, by today they would be gone.

As the sun spread light over the horizon, Gunn was able to see the trail, the woman riding a few yards ahead. Lorelei sat straight in the saddle, her left hand holding the reins snugly. Her hands were gloved. She looked, he thought, very regal.

A few bats were still out, catching the morning insects. They knifed the air on leather wings, darted off as the last few stars paled into invisibility. Gunn saw a rabbit sitting still next to a clump of mesquite, hop off lackadaisically as they passed. The sky held close under sun-tinged clouds and then even the sun disappeared so that only a gray light was cast over the land. It was quiet, peaceful.

Gunn rode up next to Lorelei.

"Your horse steps out," he said.

"So does yours."

"He have a name?"

"Amante."

"Good name. Mine's Esquire."

"Good name, too."

She looked straight ahead. He rode with her a ways, realizing that she was doing her best to ignore him. Yet she was determined. To what? To catch the men who killed her father and kill them, too? He dropped back, staying to the side, no more than a horse-length away. He wouldn't ride with her if she didn't want him to, but by God he wouldn't eat her dust either.

Her horse's name meant loving.

He wondered if she knew what the word meant.

"Don't get bitter, Billy," he told himself. Laughed quietly. His name was William Gunnison. Had been. Laurie always called him Billy. Maybe he still thought of himself as Billy now and again. But, since her death, it had been only Gunn.

A roadrunner streaked in front of them an hour later, a blur of gray and brown and white. Like an oversized magpie, silent, swift. Gunn stopped to take a leak, caught up to her, took her place a length behind to her left. An old habit. He was right-handed.

They rode through the desolate landscape of joshua trees with their uplifted arms, looking strangely human, Spanish bayonets, small cacti, sandy vistas. He realized that if he had not cut north so soon, he would have missed the desert. And Lorelei.

They stopped to water and lunch at the edge of the Anza-Borrego Desert. Even with the overcast skies, it was hot. Lorelei passed him biscuits and dried beef. They munched in silence.

Gunn built a smoke, leaned against a rock nestled against a joshua tree.

Lorelei looked at him, a longing in her deep blue eyes.

He met her glance, gave no commitment in his.

"Do you like to smoke?" she asked.

"No."

"Why do you, then?"

"It helps me think. It's something to do when I'm idle."

"What are you thinking about?"

"You. This land."

"What about me?"

"I don't know yet. You have something in your craw. I reckon."

"That doesn't sound very appealing."

"Nope. I'll live through it."

For a moment, he saw a softening in her eyes. Then they turned hard as marble.

Her lips moved and he thought she was going to say something. But she didn't. Instead, she took in a deep breath. Her breasts rose and he thought again how beautiful she was. Yet there was something big burning inside her and it would take a good man to put out that wildfire. He pinched the cigarette off, waited for her to signal she was ready to ride again. He breathed in the good air, looked at the sky. There was a lot of space here, and a man needed space. He thought that a woman might want things small, comfortable. A house, a piece of ground, a garden. Something she could handle. A man needed big things to rope. Maybe he was wrong. Lorelei didn't seem to fit, yet she looked perfectly at home. Here and back at the cabin.

A scorpion crawled toward her, its tail curled, twitching.

Lorelei didn't move, but sat perfectly still. The scorpion came up to her boot, bristled. Its tail flexed as it sidled up to the toe of her boot. Lorelei watched the creature with apparent uninterest. Then she stood up, extended her boot, stepped on the scorpion. Gunn heard its body crunch as she put her full weight on the boot.

"Shall we go?" she asked, striding toward her horse without a backward glance.

Gunn felt a sudden chill as he stood up.

Julian lay on the western edge of the Anza-Borrego Desert. Gunn and Lorelei rode in late that afternoon, her horse having picked up a thorn at a spring. In the distance, Mount Palomar jutted up over the foothills. It was cooler here. Gunn had gotten the thorn out, but the horse needed some medicants to keep the wound from festering.

"We'll put up at the livery," he said. "Horse ought to be all right by morning."

"We'll lose another day," she said, her face grim. The heat seemed to have taken some of the starch out of her, but she looked beautiful with a strand of hair falling acros her cheek.

"Save you losing a good horse."

"You're right, of course. There's a hotel here. I'll get us two rooms while you put the horses up."

So she had made it plain that she didn't want him to share her bed that night. Gunn watched her walk down the street from the livery. She looked as if she owned the town. He kicked a bale of hay as he led the horses inside the stables. No one was there. He stripped them, rubbed them down with blankets and forked hay into their stalls. Later, he would see that they got grain. He filled their water troughs, shook off the dust and headed for the Dry Gopher Saloon.

There were no horses on the street, no people. One mule stood in the shade between two clapboard buildings. A dog looked up at him from under a stall of empty crates in front.of a store. Flies buzzed and the afternoon seemed to bask in the heat like something palpable, empty. His boots boomed on the boardwalk. Glasses clinked inside the saloon. The doors were open and he felt cooler after going inside.

Men at tables looked up at him. Men at the bar pretended not to notice as he strode toward them, his shirt plastered to his body with sweat. He tipped his hat back, adjusted his eyes to the dim light. The adobe walls were sweating, but they made the saloon cool.

"Stranger," said the man behind the bar, "what'll it be?"

"The beer cold?"

"It's wet."

"Bring me a pail."

"Glass?"

"Or cup."

The bartender disappeared into the back. He was a short, squat man. Anglo, with a swooping handlebar moustache, a wad of greased hair flattened over his round skull. The hair was parted in the middle, swept back from a square face. he wore sandals and an open, buttonless shirt, the sleeves held up with garters.

"Two bits," said the man as he banged the pail on the counter. Beer sloshed.

Gunn put a quarter on the bartop.

"I'll have that glass."

"Yessir." The bartender reached behind him, grabbed a smoky glass from the back bar. He clunked it into the pail. The man seemed to like making noise.

Gunn poured beer into the glass. There was a lot of foam.

"Fresh made," said the bartender. "You passing through?"

"Yep."

"Cross the desert?"

"I did."

"Hot."

"Some." Gunn looked at the others standing at the bar. One man was old, bewhiskered, eyes as sodden as half-cooked eggs. The other was in his thirties, a Mexican, who nursed a bottle of mezcal. His eyes were red rimmed, his complexion as swarthy as leather smeared with rouge. He wore a pistol and a knife, another knife jutted out of his boot.

"Not many cross the desert this time of year. My name's Albie."

Gunn drank the beer. It was cool, tasted of clay storage. It was wet enough and it had a sharp tang to it. Better than most beer he'd tasted in better places.

"Well, Albie, I think I got lost. The Colorado was no more'n a trickle and I knew I'd come to mountains sooner or later."

"First time in California."

"First time."

"I didn't get your name."

"Gunn."

"Gun?"

"Two n's."

"Funny name."

"It's what I use."

"No offense, Gunn. We don't get many strangers through here this time of year. Prospectors, settlers . . ." His voice trailed off. He coughed self-consciously, nodded in the Mexican's direction with a knowing look.

"You must have had a pair come through here this morning. Maybe yesterday."

"Nope. Didn't see anybody different from the usual."

Gunn's interest perked.

"They'd be Chigger and Snake."

A silence seemed to draw through the room like a breath.

The Mexican swallowed a shot of mezcal.

The old timer snuffled.

A chair scraped. Gunn didn't move. His eyes narrowed and he listened hard.

Albie let out a breath.

"Oh, hell, they ain't strangers. They live here," he said.

"Here in Julian?"

"Sure do. Chigger is Manual Chigro. They call Earl Spivey 'Snake.' Don't know why. You know 'em?"

"Never met formal," said Gunn.

Albie seemed willing to talk, despite the air of tension in the saloon. Gunn swallowed more beer, liked the taste even better than he had at first. He had already learned the names of the men who killed Freddie. He was surprised, though, that the two men lived in Julian.

"You missed 'em. Spivey was in here awhile ago. Didn't see Chigger until they left. You ever see that tattoo of Spivey's? Biggest damned thing you ever saw. Got it over in Tijuana. A cactus plant with an eagle settin' on it. Now, why a man would want to paint his chest like that, I don't know. It ain't the whole eagle, just part of it, and a cactus behind it."

"Where were they headed?" asked Gunn.

"San Diego. Hey, wait a minute . . . there was a stranger here. Spivey come to meet him. Never saw the man before."

A man's voice boomed from one of the tables.

"Albie, you talk too damned much. Bring us a bottle."

Albie looked up, sheepishly, tweaked one of his moustaches.

"Sure, Ralph," said Albie. "Comin' right up."

Gunn turned, looked at the man who had spoken. He was big, red-faced, with hair to match. He looked like a prize fighter or a stevedore. A deck of cards in his hand looked like postage stamps. He wore a wide-brimmed hat, chewed on an unlit cigar.

Albie delivered the bottle. Ralph whispered something to him. Albie nodded.

When the bartender came back, Gunn knew he would say little, but there was one thing more he had to know.

"This stranger," said Gunn. "He have a name?"

Albie looked over Gunn's shoulder at Ralph. Then he bent down, began washing a glass in the sink.

"John Smith," he said, sotto voce, "and don't ask me no more questions."

Gunn finished his beer and stepped away from the bar.

He glanced at the man called Ralph.

"Just so you won't spend any time wondering," said Gunn in a loud voice. "Spider and Chigger killed Freddie Waite yesterday. They stole his gold and made his daughter an orphan. He didn't die right away and I promised him I'd do what I could."

"Mister," said Ralph, "you better learn not to make rash promises."

CHAPTER EIGHT

The Julian Hotel stood right next to the Julian Cafe, but they were separate businesses. Someone seemed to have wanted to make Julian into a town, but just naming everything Julian wasn't good enough. The place had grown about as much as it was going to, Gunn figured, and if more people didn't come soon it would die.

"Miss Waite has you in room four," said the woman at the desk. "Too bad about her father."

"And what room is Miss Waite in?" asked Gunn.

"At the other end of the hall, ten."

As far away from me as she can get, he thought.

"That'll be two dollars. Miss Waite paid for her room."

Gunn gave the matronly woman two dollars, signed his name to the register. He carried his saddlebags and rifle up the stairs, feeling them creak under his weight. No one had been at the livery stable when he returned, so he helped himself to two hatfuls of grain. Someone would be there in the morning or would ask for him at the desk, he was sure.

His room was spare, the brass bed big enough. The water pitcher was empty and the bowl was dirty. The pitcher smelled of alkali. It was hot inside, so he left the door open to air it out some. Then he walked down the hall, knocked on number ten.

"Yes?"

"It's Gunn."

"I—I'm resting."

"I've got news."

"Later. We—we'll have supper together."

Gunn thought about kicking down her door.

"Yes, ma'am," he said, and turned on his heel.

Lorelei listened to Gunn's boots reverberating on the hall floor.

She heard his door slam.

Tears welled up in her eyes. Her heart raced so that she felt faint. Her stomach quivered inside.

His voice. His footstep. His presence.

His body. His kiss.

She felt as if he was in the room with her now. Her heart beat fast just thinking about him. Her flesh tingled as if he was touching her now. She wanted him. She wanted to touch him, to nestle safe in his arms, feel his caress, his lips brush against her cheek. She wanted to feel his gentle fingers in her hair. She wanted to smell him, taste him, give herself up to him without any question in her mind.

She sat in the chair, tasting him, smelling him, wanting him. Shivering with desire.

She closed her eyes, thought of that first time. Only

74

yesterday? And she thought of the cruelty she had shown him. A good man. Better than any she'd ever seen.

The other thoughts intruded.

Her mother still spoke to her. Her aunts. She heard their voices in the silent, empty room.

"A man will use you and throw you away."

"Never trust any man."

"Hold back. Never give all of yourself to a man. A woman needs to save some of herself for her own self-respect."

"Never chase after a man. They're all no good."

"A woman who chases after a man is lost."

Lorelei put her hands up to her ears, trying to shut out the voices. She had heard them all her life. And even her father had spoken to her, echoing those other voices.

"Most men are no damned good, Lorelei. And you'll always fall for the worst. Hold back until you're sure."

How could she be sure?

Gunn might be the worst. He might be the best. There was no way of telling. But the words of her mother came back to her again, as they had after she had given herself to Gunn.

"If you're unhappy with your lot in life, darling Lorelei, you'll probably wind up marrying the first scoundrel what comes along. You'll have his babies and get his diseases and he'll leave you in the end. That's your fate if you don't read the good book and mind your p's and q's."

Nothing was ever explained.

Just the threats. The terror.

And now, Gunn.

She drew a deep breath, opened her eyes. She wished he was here in the room with her. That was shameless. Oh, she had heard a lot about shame, too. Shame was something a woman guarded herself against—at all costs.

"Don't shame yourself."

"Don't bring shame on your family."

"Don't think shameless thoughts."

"A man doesn't think about shame."

But Gunn was different. Wasn't he?

He seemed so. He seemed honest and real and wholesome, yet she wondered how her mother would have viewed him—and her aunts—her father, were he still alive. He was rough, he had no ties, no job. He was a drifter, a loner. Yet weren't most men who came West just so? Were those not the very qualities of the men who had come here first, had founded the land, opened it up to people like her and her father?

Lorelei was confused.

She wrung her hands, got up out of the chair. The fluttering had gone away. Now she was tense, irritated. Angry. Angry at herself for not knowing what to do. This was stupid. Gunn wanted her. He had shown that. But she was afraid. Afraid of what would happen now that her father was gone. She had no one to turn to anymore. Her aunts were dead or far away. Her mother was dead. She was alone.

Her instinct told her one thing, her upbringing another.

She wanted nothing more than to lie in Gunn's embrace, love him for the rest of her life.

Yet she had been warned about such feelings.

"Never let a man now you want him. He'll step all

over you."

She wanted Gunn.

She wanted to tell him how much she ached for him.

The tears welled up in her eyes as she walked to the window. She pulled up the grimy shade, looked out over the tops of the buildings toward the setting sun.

She let the tears flow. Let them wash down her cheeks and burn her flesh. Deep inside, she felt a burning, a roiling heat that she had never experienced before. Down the hall was a man. A man she wanted. He couldn't replace her father. She knew that. She didn't want another father. She wanted a man. A man like Gunn.

Yet, in her heart, she knew that all the things she had heard were true. But those words she believed were breaking her heart. She knew that as well. She wanted only to give herself to Gunn.

But she was afraid.

Mortally afraid.

The man who tended the livery stable looked up as Gunn's shadow fell on him. He saw the silhouette of a big man in the doorway, stood up, leaned on the shovel in his hand.

"*Buenas,*" said the man.

"*Buenas tardes,*" said Gunn. He walked over to the black's stall, lifted the left forefoot. He pulled out a tin of salve, began working it into the thorn wound under the shoe. The Mexican watched him.

"You know horses."

"Some."

"I am Enrique Cardenas. This is my little stable."

"It is a good stable, Enrique. I want to pay you for boarding these two horses. I have given them hay and some grain."

"Yes, I know. Three dollars, maybe two."

Gunn laughed. He set the horse's hoof down gently, clamped the lid back on the tin, stuck it in his shirt. He gave Enrique three dollars.

"Thank you. You are the one they talk about. You are called Gunn."

"I am."

"They say Manuel he killed Freddie Waite."

"He did."

"And Snake was killing him, too."

"He was in on it."

"They are bad men, but there are a lot of bad men. You will kill them when you find them?"

"If I have to. They are thieves, too."

"Yes. *Ladrones. Bandidos.* But you have another worry, *señor*. In this town, you have a shadow. You have talked with this man, I think."

"Ralph something."

Cardenas moved closer. He was a corpulent man. His belly sagged over his waistband. He had a thin moustache, short sideburns, a face like a harvest moon, ruddy from the mixed blood of his ancestors and raw from the sun and wind. He was losing his teeth.

"This is a dangerous man. *Muy peligroso*. His name is Ralph Kimmons. He is a friend to Snake Spivey."

"I will keep my eyes open for Kimmons."

"It is not only this one, but his companion. He has killed many men and he has done it so quick and easy most of them did not know they were going to meet their maker."

78

"And who is this man?"

"Oh, but you must have seen him. he is always nearby Kimmons. That is how they do it. Torres, he was there when you saw Kimmons."

"Torres. He a slender Mexican, skinny, wearing the Californio pants, carries a knife stuck in his boot?"

"Yes. He carries knives in both boots and on his belt and in another place."

Gunn nodded.

"He was drunk."

"Do not be too sure, *amigo*. He always looks that way and he is an actor. He pretends fear and his eyes weep as if he had been drinking too much mezcal. But he has a hollow leg and he can drink much. He is very quick with the pistol and with the blade. He is the shadow of the shadow who follows you and you must watch him more carefully than you do the gringo, eh?"

"I understand. Why are you telling me this?"

"Because Chigro, he ruined my sister. He made her into a whore. And because I would like to kill him myself."

"Do you know the man they met?"

Cardenas shook his head.

"But you saw him?"

"I saw him. They said his name was John Smith, but that is not his name. I have seen him before. In Ramona, I think. Or El Cajon. Somewhere."

Gunn tried to quell his excitement.

"Do you know his profession? Where he lives?"

"No. He might own some gold mines and he might be an *abogado*."

"A lawyer."

"Yes. He is in some kind of business and he has

79

money. No one knows very much about these men. But you are going to San Diego and you will find out much. Be careful when you go to Ramona because it is said that . . ."

Cardenas stopped talking suddenly. His eyes went wide. Gunn turned, saw a shape flash by the doorway. he heard a hissing sound, followed by a dull thunk.

Cardenas sighed deeply.

Gunn whirled, caught the man as he fell.

A knife jutted from square between the Mexican's shoulder blades.

Bile rose up in Gunn's throat.

He jerked the knife free, wincing as he saw the width of the blade, the length. It was one of those Mexican knives like the one he carried, only larger. It was copied from a bowie—sharp on both sides of the blade. When it went into a man it cut through veins, arteries, anything in its way. This one was honed to a razor-sharp edge. It was slick with blood.

Gunn lay the wounded man down.

"Is there a *medico* here?" he asked.

Cardenas wheezed. Blood bubbled out of his mouth, pink and frothy. The blade had punctured a lung. Probably severed an artery leading to the heart. The Mexican was bleeding inside. He was dying.

The horses, as if sensing death, nickered softly.

Cardenas closed his eyes, shuddered. His throat made a rattling sound. He expelled a brief breath and did not draw in another.

Gunn set the man's head down, stood up. He wiped the wet blade on his trousers, shoved it in his belt. The handle was made from an elk's antler. Like the one he'd seen in Torres' boot.

But there had been two men.

The one who raced by the front door was only a decoy. Torres had been waiting at the back door.

Gunn was almost certain that Ralph Kimmons had been the man he'd seen. He had never seen Torres at all. In fact, he could not even identify Kimmons as the man who had dashed past the front door of the livery stable.

A shadow.

And Torres, the shadow of a shadow.

CHAPTER NINE

The Julian Cafe was closed.

The Dry Gopher was closed.

The town was all shuttered and the stillness was eerie.

When Gunn and Lorelei returned to the hotel, no one was at the desk. A single lamp burned, but the wick was turned low.

"Gunn, what's happening? I—I'm frightened."

"We'll eat hardtack and jerky," he said softly. Even so, his voice echoed in the empty lobby. The streets of Julian were dark. Full of shadows. "Come, we'll make do, leave early in the morning."

"I've never seen the town shut down like this."

"No. Someone is scared."

"Everyone is scared, if you ask me. Does it have anything to do with Enrique?"

He had told her about the murder.

"It has to do with us, too. Come. We make good targets here."

He hurried her up the stairs, unlocked his door.

Lorelei was trembling when he touched her arm. He lit a lamp, pulled the shades. He rummaged through his saddle bags, found the hardtack and jerky.

"I—I'm not hungry," she said.

"You need something on your stomach."

"I knew Enrique. He was a gentle man. He never hurt a soul."

"Did you know his sister?"

"No. Why?"

"Nothing. He mentioned her, that's all."

"Gunn, this is frightening. What's happening? Surely the whole town wouldn't turn against us? Against me? I was here only two days ago."

"Freddie was alive then. Lorelei, I think we've stumbled onto something bigger than a killing and robbery. There are people here who know something and don't want to know anything. They're hiding like rabbits when the hawk is flying."

"I don't understand."

"Neither do I. Yet."

Gunn chewed his food slowly, thoughtfully. He drank water from his canteen. Lorelei could not be persuaded to eat. She lay on the bed, fell asleep. He built a smoke, stayed away from the windows. He was not sleepy. His nerves jangled. He listened to every sound in the hotel. There were few, and these only from the settling of the building as the night turned chilly. He heard no sound on the street. It was as if the world had suddenly emptied of people and they were the only two left on Earth.

He looked at Lorelei. Her face was ashen, drained of blood. She looked beautiful in repose. Now he had seen still another side of her. She was frightened. Frightened of things she could not see. That was the worst fear—the fear of the unknown, of forces beyond any man's control. She had been through a lot and anyone would be unsettled over such extraordinary events. No wonder she had seemed cold and distant. She was packing a lot of hard goods on her shoulders. He wanted to take her in his arms, stroke her hair, tell her that everything would be all right.

But everything wasn't all right.

There were two killers out there, waiting to strike again.

Someone was going to a lot of trouble to make sure Snake and Chigger got away clean.

He couldn't blame the whole town. But someone, someone bigger than those two, or Torres and Kimmons, was calling the shots.

Who?

He was convinced that even Cardenas hadn't known. But he might have had an inkling. He seemed on the point of telling Gunn more when he was murdered. Now the trail was about to go cold. Whatever Cardenas might have told him was lost forever. He would have to follow the leads himself. If he lived long enough.

Gunn woke from a deep sleep, someone shaking him.

He opened his eyes to darkness.

"There's someone here," said Lorelei. He felt her hands on his shoulders. Her face was hidden in shadow. He saw her shape, heard her whisper. "Are you awake?"

He shook off the sleepiness.

"What is it?"

"Listen."

Gunn heard it.

A board creaked outside the door. There was a metallic sound.

Someone was picking the lock.

Gunn rose from his bedroll on the floor, strapped on his gunbelt. He found Lorelei's face in the dark, put a finger over her lips. He walked barefooted to the door. He found the key, gripped it carefully. He heard breathing on the other side of the door.

He looked for Lorelei, saw her shape by the bed.

There was no time to warn her. He would have to move fast, take his chances she would not be hurt.

The lock rattled again. The floorboards creaked.

Gunn turned the key quickly, jerked open the door.

The explosion rocked him to his heels. Hot powder scorched his face. White smoke enveloped him, choked him. His eyes stung from the flash, the hot peppers of burning black powder. He ducked, regained his balance, and charged through the doorway.

Lorelei screamed.

Gunn smacked into someone, felt flesh, cloth. His eyes ached inside his lids. He was blind. His ears rang, muffled all sounds. He heard the man he struck grunt, felt his body give way.

Something hard struck him on the shoulder. Something metal. A sharp pain reverberated through his shoulder blade. His back muscles flared with agony. He kept driving, found himself falling as the man's legs gave way. The two slammed into the opposite wall.

Gunn was at a disadvantage. He couldn't see. He could only sense where the man's face was. He held on, loosed his right hand, cocked it quick and drove it straight toward the sound of the man's breathing. His knuckles crunched into bone. He felt something squirt onto his hand. His knuckles stung, went numb. The man he hit cursed, brought a knee up into Gunn's groin.

Gunn's stomach went sick as the pain spread from his testicles. He doubled over, losing his grip on the man he could not see.

Lorelei yelled a warning from inside the room.

"Look out, Gunn!"

He opened his burning eyes.

Shadowy shapes danced before him, blurred by tears.

Something hard cracked into his skull.

He reached out blindly, grabbed at the bulky shape before him. His hands touched cloth. He jerked, felt something rip. He heard a sound like cloth tearing. A boot landed in his gut. He fell back. His hand came away clean, clutching a fragment of shirt.

A shot boomed in his ear.

He heard the ball sizzle past his head, raising the hackles on the back of his neck.

Gunn rolled, clawed for his own pistol. He drew it, cocked it.

"Damnit, he's gonna shoot!" a man shouted.

Gunn shot.

He shot at the voice. He shot out of pain, out of frustration, out of blindness. He didn't want to shoot, but he knew he was a dead man if he didn't. He shot out of instinct and a hard self-discipline. He shot because he wanted to kill instead of be killed.

Boots scuffed on the floor. A body crashed against the wall. Gunn kept rolling, firing high. He heard a grunt, garbled curses. Lorelei, in the room, gasped and he heard her as if she was whispering in his ear. Every sound was intensified, magnified. Smoke clogged his nostrils. His face stung from hot powder. His nuts swelled as if spitted over an open fire. His stomach churned with nausea, with the sickness of the pain that flooded his body.

He heard men stumbling down the stairs.

Then, the silence.

Gunn opened his tear-filled eyes. Panic gripped him as he realized he was blind.

He groped for a wall. His hand clutched empty air. Off balance, disoriented, he fell over. His body fell heavily on the floor.

"Gunn, are you hurt?"

He groped for the wall, again, touched it. He crawled toward it, slid up to a standing position. His eyes strained to see through a dark haze. He saw only nothingness, a blur that had no definition.

"Damnit, I'm blind," he rasped.

Lorelei gasped, ran to him. The smoke hung in the air like a pall. He heard her footsteps, felt her hand on his arm. He stared hard, trying to see her face.

"Did they shoot you?" she asked, her voice quivering with dread.

"No."

A wave of nausea engulfed him. The blindness made him claustrophobic. His stomach grew queasy as he hugged the wall, felt as though he was standing over a deep pit.

"Come," she said. "We'll go to my room. They might come back."

"Yes." He felt vulnerable, exposed. She led him down the hall. He stumbled, cursing his sightlessness. She leaned him against something. A wall.

"Wait here. I forgot my key. I—I'll lock your room. Don't worry. You'll be all right."

Her hand went away. He heard her footsteps retreat down the hall. He tried to remember how many shots he had fired. His pistol was a dead weight in his hand, useless. His arm hung down and he leaned his face against the wall, closed his eyes. They ached. Something behind them ached. His head throbbed where he had been struck. But the pain was bearable. The blindness was not. A lump rose in his throat. Spidery sensations crawled through his stomach.

There was something in his left hand, too. A scrap of cloth. He shoved it in his pocket. He could not see it. He could not see anything. And in the blindness was something else. Something that made his insides shake as if he was riding a bucking bronc.

Gunn knew what it was.

It was fear.

Lorelei led Gunn to a chair.

"There was a lot of blood in the hall," she said.

"Did you see the men?"

"No."

Gunn said nothing. He was pretty sure the two men had been Torres and Kimmons. He had wounded one of them, maybe both. How badly, he did not know. But they had meant to kill him. They had come for him, knowing he would be there. Even the hotel was deserted. All those shots fired and no one even curious.

He heard Lorelei walking around the room. He heard the tinkle of glass, the scratch of a match on sandpaper. He thought he could feel the glow of the lamp, but knew it was only his imagination. His eyes still ached and were sodden with tears. He felt dizzy, dislocated. His head throbbed and he wanted to go to sleep. A bad sign, he knew. He probably had a concussion. He'd have to ride it out. He fought against the temptation to let himself drift off.

He listened, heard the rustle of cloth. The bedsprings creaked with weight. Then something clunked on the floor. The springs creaked again as weight was released. He heard the pad of bare feet.

"Lorelei?"

"Yes?"

"What are you doing?"

She didn't answer, but he heard her come near.

Fingers worked at the buttons of his shirt. His belt buckle. He pushed her away, suddenly angry.

His hands touched naked flesh.

"Are you crazy, Lorelei?"

"Yes," she whispered. "I want you, Gunn."

"I can't even see you. That lamp's going to tell those men right where we are."

He felt her hands tugging on his trousers, pulling them down his legs.

"I'll blow it out," she whispered.

"Damnit, woman, I don't understand you."

She went away and the glass tinkled again. He knew

the room was dark. He heard her come back. The floor-boards creaked in front of him.

Something soft brushed against his legs. He felt them being pried apart. Before he realized what was happening, he felt a wetness, a warmth. A tongue.

Lorelei's mouth.

CHAPTER TEN

Ralph Kimmons sagged to the cot, his leg drenched with blood.

Torres loosed his grip on the big man.

"Jesus, he done me good."

"No, it is not a bad wound. Wait."

Torres brought the lamp close, set it on a crate that served as a table. He drew a knife, deftly slit Kimmons' trouser leg. He looked at the exposed wound. Gunn's bullet had plowed a furrow through the thick flesh of the man's thigh. The bullet had gone clean through.

"Well?"

Torres walked to the table, picked up a bottle of tequila. He jerked the cork with his teeth. He walked back over to the cot, poured the alcohol directly into the open wound. Kimmons swore, winced with pain.

"You bastard."

Torres grinned.

He bandaged the wound with a shirt he tore up.

"I'll have some of that tequeely," said Kimmons. Torres gave him the slender bottle. Kimmons drank as

Torres tied the knot tight.

"You're shutting off my blood."

"Tomorrow, you pack this with unguent."

"We got to get him, Torres."

"Not tonight."

"No, damnit, not tonight."

"He is blind now. He will be easy."

"He was blind when he shot me."

Torres walked across the room, stood by the window. The shack was outside of town. Two cots, a cheap stove, some crates for chairs, a table. A hideout. Just in case Gunn came after them. He looked out the window at the silver-dusted land. There was no movement, no sound. The horses were put up in a kind of lean-to in back of the jacal, silently nibbling on hay.

"He is dangerous, that one," said Torres, slipping his knife back in its scabbard.

"Hell, he's just a man. Lucky."

"No, not that one. He is not lucky. He is sure."

"I don't follow you, Torres."

Torres turned from the window, sat on a crate. The lamp flickered with bad oil, smoked up the chimney so that the room seemed to grow shadows.

"Man like that, he don't follow the same road you pick for him. He's harder to kill than a wild boar or a cat. You jump one way, he jumps the other. You follow him, pretty soon he is following you. And something is following him all the time."

"Huh?"

Torres looked up at Kimmons as if he had suddenly remembered the man was there. The Mexican seemed lost in thought.

"Oh, nothing. It is just a saying among my people."

Kimmons sat up, cradling the bottle in his arm. He winced with pain.

"Damnit, I want to hear about it."

Torres looked away, stared at a wall as if he could see beyond it.

"They say there are men like that. With the *sombra.*"

"The what?"

"*Sombra.* A shadow following them. Maybe protecting them."

"You got bats in your belfry, Torres."

Torres sighed.

"Yes, perhaps. But this man is different. He will not lie down and he will not go away."

"You sound as though you admire the jasper."

"No. But maybe I am a little afraid of him."

Kimmons laughed. His laugh sounded hollow in the room.

"You ain't afraid of nothin', hoss."

Torres got up, restless. He walked to the door, stood there, just staring into nothingness. Kimmons watched him with narrowed eyes.

"Best you turn in, Torres," he said. "That Gunn's blinded, he'll be easy pickin's come mornin'."

"We will get up early, eh?"

"Early, before the quails."

"I am thinking that if we don't kill this man tomorrow he will kill us and then go after Snake and Chigger."

"Well, that's what we're gettin' paid fer. So's this jasper don't ever reach San Diego."

Torres walked over to the other cot. He lay down without taking off his boots or his gunbelt. He threw an arm over his face. The wick would burn down soon, but

he was glad there was some light. His thoughts were ..
dark enough and he had an uneasy feeling about
tomorrow. He listened to Kimmons swig on the
tequila and wondered if he, too, wasn't just a little
afraid.

Gunn lay naked in bed, exhausted, bewildered.

Lorelei, finally, was asleep.

She had devoured him, wanted him with a despera-
tion he had never seen in a woman before. As if her life
depended on his coupling with her. His skin tingled all
over from her ravishing kisses, her plucking hands. She
seemed insatiable. He had heard stories of such
women, but never given them much credence. He could
not remember the word that they were called, but men
talked of them with leers on their faces and laughed
about them, expressing the wish that they could find
such a woman before their days were over.

Was Lorelei such a woman?

Gunn did not know.

She was distraught. A lot had happened to her. She
had a frailer constitution than he would have thought.
One moment she seemed bold and aggressive, the next
she was hostile or fearful. She was a complex woman,
he granted her that. Beyond any explanation he might
have.

And she was beautiful, a fine lover.

But what drove her?

Tonight he had been her prisoner. Was, still. He
could not see. His head throbbed as though a landslide
rumbled down the slopes of his brain. The ringing in his
ears had gone away, replaced with a faint buzzing. He

wondered if he would ever see again.

He had not seen her tonight. Instead, he had felt her, listened to her hoarse whispers, tasted her hot, wet kisses all over his body. He felt strange, now, as if he had dreamed it all.

Yet he knew it had happened. He had never seen such raw lust in a woman. But there was also a reserve there, too, a shame that seemed to be just beneath the surface. She turned hot and cold and there was no way of telling when she would change. She kept him off balance, unsure of himself. He didn't like the feeling. He didn't like seeing her go through those wild changes of mood. There was no way to reach her, talk to her, find out why she behaved so. When she wanted him, she swept him up in her passion. When she turned against him, rejected him, he felt as though the sky had gone black, building for a storm coming from a long way off.

There was a darkness in Lorelei's heart. It made him sad to see it. He saw it better now that he was blind. For he had felt the same way himself, once. Grief. It sawed at a man. It cut parts of him out and scattered them to the four directions. And, sometimes, it took a long time to find them, put them back where they belonged.

Lorelei was driven by something she couldn't understand.

Outwardly, she appeared to be a kind of madwoman, haunted by vagrant lusts that overpowered her—and him. Inside, he knew, there was a sweet, normal woman. But she was a woman lost, as he had been lost once. And in his blindness, while he could see clearly, he could not reach her, could not help her.

Nor could he help himself.

For in spite of the way she acted toward him, in spite of the things she did that put a burr under his blanket, a kink in his spine, he was drawn to her, wanted her. He wanted her so much it scared him.

And his own shame was deeper than hers, for when she came to him, he did not run away, as he should.

He took her, knowing all the time that it was the other way around.

Lorelei was the savage.

He was the slave.

She straddled him, rubbing her female parts against his bulging crotch.

Gunn sat up, opened his eyes.

He cringed inwardly, realizing that it was not the dark he saw. He saw nothing.

Lorelei's breathing came in gasps. Her hands kneaded his flesh as if she was making dough.

Gunn lashed out blindly, his hands seeking her shoulders. He felt bare skin, clutched her hard. He held on, shoved her from his body. He twisted, pinning her to the bed.

"What time is it?" he growled.

"I—I don't know. Let loose. You're hurting me."

"Is it dark outside?"

"Yes."

"Morning?"

"Close to morning. Gunn—Gunn don't do this. I can't help myself. I woke up, felt your body next to mine. I'm burning up. All over."

His brows wrinkled with the strain of his thoughts. He quelled the anger rising up in him.

"Listen, you little bitch," he said tightly, "if I wasn't half crazy about you, I'd wring your neck. I'm blind, and there are men out there looking to blow holes in me." His hands squeezed her shoulders. Hard. "I'd love to romp with you every time you snap your fingers, but unless we get moving before dawn, we'll both wind up six feet under. Savvy?"

"You're hurting me."

His hands slipped down to her neck.

"Make your choice, Lorelei. Get me dressed, saddle our horses and lead me out of here or I'll squeeze until you turn blue and I'll keep squeezing until you don't ever breathe again."

"Gunn, are you . . . serious?"

"I'm serious."

"You—you'd kill me?"

"They'll kill you if I don't. Right now, you're my biggest problem. You can be my eyes and we'll get out of this. Or you can screw me silly and they'll just put lead in us while we're humping like a couple of alley cats."

"Is—is that what you think of me, of what we've had together?"

Gunn's hands tightened around her neck. His whole body tightened.

"Shut up, Lorelei. Just shut the hell up and make your choice."

He released her, climbed from her body.

His hands shook.

His whole body trembled.

He sat on the edge of the bed and fought back the feeling of self-pity, the loathing that crawled over him. He wanted to smash something. Anything. He wanted

97

to tear up the room he could not see and he wanted to drive his fists into someone's face.

He was blind.

He was helpless, frustrated.

He hated.

The silence stretched for a long time.

The bed creaked as Lorelei moved.

Gunn tensed, listening. He shut his eyes tightly as if to squeeze out the pain behind them, as if to bring the light back.

"Gunn," she whispered. "I'm sorry. Truly. I didn't think of you. I just . . ."

He rose up, stood there, shaking his head, afraid to take a step because he might fall.

"Don't say any more," he said gruffly. "Just get us out of here. Maybe I can find a doc and . . ."

"Yes," she agreed, her voice still hushed. "We must go."

Her voice choked off and he heard her stifle a sob. There was a woman there in the room. He ached for her, but he ached for life even more.

He felt like a child as she helped him dress. When they finally left the hotel, he had to be led by the hand. At the livery stable, he listened as Lorelei saddled their mounts. Leather creaked, the horses were jumpy and tried to avoid being cinched up.

"Is it still dark out?" he wanted to know.

"Yes. The horses are ready. I'll help you up when we get outside."

"Saddlebags? My rifle?"

"Everything is ready. It's starting to get light."

"Where next?"

"Ramona There's a doc there. Maybe he can help you."

Her voice was soft. There was a tenderness to her words. Outside, she helped him get his boot into the stirrup, guided his hand to the saddle horn. Gunn swung up, swayed off balance as he fought to discern his bearings. A moment later, he heard her mount.

"Give me one of your reins until we get out of town," she said.

"Lorelei, I'm damned sorry about this."

"You can't help it. I just hope you're not . . ."

"Permanently blind?"

"Yes," she said tightly.

She took a rein; Gunn held onto the saddle horn

"Anybody following us?" he asked.

"I don't know. I don't see anybody."

"Where are we now?"

"Just passing the hotel. I'm going to go a little faster. Hold on."

"I'm not a baby," he snapped.

"Yes, you are, Gunn. But I'm not going to mother you. I still want to catch those men and if you're not able to keep up, I'll leave you in Ramona."

He knew from the sound of her words that she meant it.

Inside, he began to ache for her again.

Sightless or seeing, Gunn knew that he would go to hell for Lorelei. No matter how she treated him.

CHAPTER ELEVEN

Harvey Gold watched the strange couple ride up to his house. Through the window, he saw what appeared to be a normal, healthy man being led on horseback by someone he knew. Lorelei Waite. But she was tight-lipped, her face frozen to a mask. The man he did not recognize, but something was wrong with him. When they dismounted, he saw the man wait as she tied the horses' reins to the hitchrail. Then she took him by the shoulders, led him up the steps. He reached out ahead of him, like a blind man.

Gunn's eyes smarted from the sun. He wiped tears from his cheek, heard his boots ring hollow on the porch.

"This is Doc Gold's house," she explained.

The sign hanging from the porch eaves said that Gold was a surgeon, dentist and physician.

He opened the door.

"Lorelei."

"Harvey."

Gold was a short-statured, beefy man with mutton chops, pince-nez on his prominent nose. His eyes were brown, his teeth uneven, stained with tobacco from smoking the pipe that seemed to grow out of the corner of his mouth. His bushy eyebrows were starting to gray and needed trimming. They jutted out at all angles as though two caterpillars had taken up residence on his forehead.

"Come in. What seems to be the trouble?"

Lorelei coughed, helped Gunn through the door. He had to duck, after the crown of his hat brushed the top of the opening.

"Can't see," said Gunn.

"Bring him into my office, Lorelei," said Gold.

Lorelei guided Gunn to a chair in another room. The chair was hard, creaked under his weight. She held onto his shoulders to keep him from falling until he was settled straight. He heard the doctor's voice from a few feet away.

"How long have you been unable to see?" asked Gold.

"Since last night."

"How'd it happen?" Gunn heard the sound of the shades being pulled.

"Gunpowder."

Lorelei's hands slipped off his shoulders. He heard her take a few steps, sit on something soft. The divan, or chair, made a wheezing sound.

Gold moved a chair close to Gunn. The feet scraped on the floor.

"I'm going to examine you," said Gold. His voice shifted to a professional tone—soft, authoritative. "If it hurts, you tell me."

"What do you think, Harvey?" asked Lorelei.

"Nothing, yet."

Gunn felt a finger touch his head. He winced.

"You take a fall, too?"

"I got hit."

"Yes. Nasty bruise under the skin. Soft, pulpy. I'm going to look at your eyes now. Might hurt some."

Gunn heard a match strike. The doctor opened one eye, then the other. Gunn felt the heat from the flame.

"See anything?"

"A light. Dim."

"Describe it to me."

"Far away, like a January sun. Pale, no bigger than a pinhead."

"All right." Gold blew out the flame.

Gunn heard the doctor's chair groan as he shifted position.

"Your eyes hurt when they're closed?"

"They sting some."

"Hmmm."

A chair leg scraped. Footsteps sounded on a rug that he could not see. Gunn listened to Lorelei's breathing, from somewhere behind him. A cabinet door creaked. Water gurgled out of a container. The footsteps came close again. Gold did not sit down. Gunn felt his presence. Close.

"I'm going to put a weak solution in your eyes," said the doctor. "It'll burn some. If there are traces of gunpowder in there, this should wash them out. Then I want you to close your eyes for about five minutes."

"All right," said Gunn.

Gunn felt the doctor's strong fingers pry open an eyelid. Something liquid ran into his eye. It burned. He closed it. Gold opened the other eye. Again, the burning.

"Tight shut, now," said Gold.

After a few moments, the burning went away. Lorelei got up. He heard her walk out of the room with Gold.

They stopped, not quite out of earshot.

"How's Freddie?" said Gold.

"He—he was killed. Gunn there is helping me track the men who did it."

"You know who it was?"

"Chigger . . . and Snake."

Gunn heard the doctor suck in a breath.

"Christ," he said. "Snake."

"Yes," she said tightly. "Spivey."

There was a pause as Gunn strained to hear.

"You plan on seeing Bobbie?"

"No," she said quickly. "I—I can't."

The doctor's tone lowered, but Gunn could still hear.

"The widow Ross has taken good care of him."

"Please, Harvey . . . not now. I—I know she has. I just can't face that now."

"You don't hate the boy."

"No . . . it's not his fault. It's just that I have things to work out."

"Stay away from Snake, Lorelei. You can't change the past."

"He—I should have killed him a long time ago. Then none of this would have happened."

Gunn heard her begin to sob. Feet scuffled on

the floor.

"I'm going to give you a sedative. I'm sorry about Freddie. I'll miss him. You can lie down in the parlor, collect your thoughts."

The footsteps went away. Gold came back, opened a cabinet, then walked out of the room again. Gunn's eyes stopped burning. He wondered what that conversation was all about. From the sound of it, Lorelei had had dealings with Snake before. And who was Bobbie? And the widow Ross? More puzzles.

"You can open your eyes now, Mister Gunn."

The doctor's voice startled him. He had dozed off and Gold had tiptoed back into the office.

Gunn opened his eyes. He saw a shape, the doctor, through a watery film.

"See anything?"

"A blur."

"Good. In a few minutes I'll put some ointment in there. By tonight, you ought to be back to normal."

"Tonight?"

"We mustn't rush these things. The cornea's probably scratched. I looked at your eyes under a magnifying glass. Doesn't appear to be much damage, if any. Could be your poor eyesight is due to another cause."

"Such as?"

"Oh," said Gold lightly, "such a condition could be caused by a blow to the head or . . ."

"Or what?"

"Or some emotional disturbance. A strain."

Gunn closed his eyes, blinked out the tears. A buzzing in his ears started up, and he wondered if the doctor might not be partly right. Lorelei had upset some kind of balance in him. The doctor, he decided, was a pretty smart man.

"What do I owe you, doc?"

"Oh, two dollars ought to cover it. You just sit tight for a spell. I'll check your eyes again in a few minutes. Right now, I'd like to talk, if you've a mind to—about Lorelei."

"Lorelei?" Gunn's throat tightened.

"Yes. Have you known her long?"

"Just met her. I was there when her father—Freddie—was killed."

"You saw it happen?"

Gunn told him about it. He didn't tell him about Lorelei. Not what had happened between them.

"Terrible thing to happen just now," said Gold.

"Yes. Terrible anytime."

"What's your interest in Lorelei, Mister Gunn?"

Blunt. To the point. Gunn opened his eyes again. He could barely discern the doctor's features, his slightly bulging eyes, his nose, mouth.

"I don't know. I made a promise to her father before he died."

"So, you're helping her go after Snake?"

"And Chigger."

The doctor shook his head. He put his fingers to the bridge of his nose, squeezed and kneaded the bone. He drew a deep breath.

"Maybe I shouldn't tell you this. If Lorelei hasn't, then she probably doesn't want you to know. But you'll find out anyway, if . . ."

"Don't tell him!"

Lorelei stood in the doorway, hanging onto it as if to

keep from falling. Gunn could barely see her shadowy figure. Her voice was sharp, cutting.

"Lorelei, don't be silly. It's obvious that this man cares about you. You can't just shoulder this all by yourself."

"Just shut up, Harvey. I don't want you butting in on my business. It—it isn't what you think. Gunn is just . . ."

She broke off. The doctor looked down at his shoes self-consciously.

"Just what?" said Gunn evenly.

"Just . . . nothing. I just don't want you to know my business, that's all. Harvey, you should learn to respect my privacy."

Gold stood up, went to her. Gunn closed his eyes against the strain. He heard them, though.

"Lorelei," said Gold, "I wouldn't hurt you for the world. You know that. But you're all alone now. You need friends. You need . . ."

"I need nothing," she snapped. Then, turning to Gunn, she said, "I'm leaving this afternoon. With or without you."

"I'll be ready," said Gunn.

Gold shuffled back to his cabinet, a table. He searched through the cabinet for an apothecary jar, found it. He took a cotton swab, dipped it into the opened container. He came over to Gunn, peeled back an eyelid.

"This won't hurt, but it'll feel lumpy. Just relax."

The doctor applied the ointment delicately, closed the eye. He did the same procedure with the other eye. When he was finished, he wrapped a gauze bandage around Gunn's head, covering both eyes.

"I feel like I'm going to an execution," said Gunn, as Gold tied a knot in the bandage.

No one said a word.

Gunn pulled his hat brim down low over his face to shield the blindfold.

Lorelei led him from the boarding stable to the Rancho El Cajon, a hospitality house with a cantina, El Monterrey, adjoining. The afternoon sun beat down; flies buzzed; dogs dozed.

"I've decided to stay over," she said, as she checked them in, "leave early in the morning. There's something I want to do. I probably won't be back until late."

"Separate rooms."

"Yes. Here, people would talk."

Gunn understood. He wondered, though, at the sinking feeling in his stomach, the indefinable ache that had no location. It seemed to be centered at first in one place, then another. The darkness didn't help. He wanted to look into her eyes, see her face. He wanted to ask her things that he had never asked a woman before. He wanted to kiss her, to hold her close, to feel her breasts against his chest. He wanted her to lie with him and be his woman.

He was surprised to hear her speak Spanish to the clerk. Good Spanish. He stood there, his head bowed so his bandage wouldn't show. He felt helpless. He carried his saddlebags and rifle, but they seemed like useless lumps in his hands. He felt disoriented, lost. He had no bearings, for the first time in his life. He didn't know where he was. He was under the complete control of a woman he didn't understand. A cold, hard woman, who could be tender and soft. A woman who was two women and he didn't know either one of them.

"It's a nice room," she said, upstairs. "Cool. Are you hungry?"

"No. I can pull on some jerky."

"Don't pout, Gunn."

"I'm not pouting."

She laughed, mockingly, and he winced. He wanted to tear the blindfold off and wrestle her to his will. He sensed the bed in the room, wished that he were lying on it, and she in his arms.

"Sit here, and I'll describe the room to you."

"Where are you going, Lorelei?" His voice sounded alien to him, croaky, scratchy with fear. It was probably so. He was afraid. But he did not know what he was afraid of and that made the fear worse.

She laughed again and he could not deny the sting.

"To see some people. Look, Gunn, I can't just nurse you. I'm giving you an extra day. Chigro and Snake will go to San Diego, if they're not here, and then they'll be back. I want to see them dead, like my father is dead, but we've lost the day. You'll have to fend for yourself while I'm gone."

"I will."

"Yes, I'm sure you will."

Did her voice quaver? Did she care about him? He couldn't tell. He could not see her face. He could only hear the harsh edge to her voice, the cutting tone that knifed him in that aching place that had no certain location.

He sat there, listening to her describe the objects in

the room.

When she left, she kissed him on the cheek. The kiss was almost motherly.

The door slammed.

Lorelei was gone and the room was empty.

Gunn was empty.

·

CHAPTER TWELVE

The minutes dragged by, became hours.

Gunn found his way to the bed, slept. He did not dream, but neither did he sleep deep nor well. He sweated, tossed, dozed.

When he awoke, the room was quiet and the street outside was quiet. He listened for familiar sounds and there was only his breathing. The blindfold was loose around his eyes and the relative coolness of the air made him think that it might be night.

He felt the bed to see if Lorelei had returned.

He knew she hadn't.

His eyes itched and he clawed at the bandage.

He jerked it over his head, tossed it to the floor. He kept his eyes shut tight, wondering if the medicine Doc Gold had given him would work. He hesitated, mildly afraid to open his eyes.

Could he face blindness? Total blindness? For the rest of his days? He gave it some thought. A man could do anything he set his mind to. A man could live with most anything. After the war, he had seen the wounded soldiers, the maimed, with their wooden stumps, those with patches over blown-out eyes, those giddy with a nameless addlement from the sound of cannon and the whip of grapeshot flicking over a battleground crawling with screaming men. He had seen those with empty eyes who sat on town porches staring at nothing although their eyes could see.

Slowly, Gunn opened his eyes.

The room was dark, and a rush of disappointment flooded his senses. Then, he began to perceive shapes, a glimmer of light outside the window. He walked to the window, looked down at the street below. A slow smile creased his face as he saw a mule standing hipshot at the hitchrail, a cone of golden light from a wagon lantern spilling on the street. A man rummaged through a buckboard, finally came up with a keg. He hefted the keg, blew out the lantern and walked up the street, disappearing from view.

Gunn felt the soft spot on his skull. The tenderness was mostly gone. His eyes felt fine, although there was mucous at the corners. He took his bandanna from his pocket, dabbed the matter away. He did not light a lamp, but checked his Colt, felt his beard. Scratchy, but it would do. His stomach rattled and gurgled with hunger. He wanted a drink.

He drew a breath, felt a great weight lift from his shoulders.

He was alive. He could see again.

He found the key Lorelei had left for him on the table, walked to the door, opened it. He could hear the sounds of people in El Monterrey downstairs. Laughter, the tinkle of glasses, a plaintive guitar. People. Life. He closed the door, locked it, tucked the key in his pocket.

He wondered where Lorelei was, when she would return. He couldn't wait to see her. Part of his hunger, he knew, was not for food, but for her.

Ethel Ross was a small, exuberant woman with merry, blue-green eyes, curly gray hair, rosy cheeks among the wrinkles on her face. Life had not daunted her, but made her only more determined to enjoy it, despite the losses and hardships she had endured. She lived on a hill, surrounded by her goats and chickens, pet quail that she kept in cages, and a milk cow that she kept fresh by selling the calves she bore. She sat in a rocking chair, knitting by lamplight, while Lorelei looked at the collection of bugs, dead frogs, and lizards that little Bobbie had spread out on the floor.

"I'm glad you came, dearie," said Mrs. Ross. "I liked it a lot better when Bobbie collected pretty rocks."

Lorelei laughed, a slight nervousness apparent in her demeanor. Bobbie, a dark-haired tad of five, looked at her adoringly. He had her startling blue eyes, her hair and his grandfather's mouth. His nose and facial structure harked back to another progenitor, his father.

"Mommy," he said, "I saw a turtle today. But it runned away."

"Ran," said Lorelei, smiling.

"Ranned."

Ethel chuckled.

Lorelei had not told her about Freddie yet. She didn't want to spoil the few hours she had. Bobbie had asked for "Gan-pa" several times, and she had avoided his questions. Freddie was away, that was all she said. But Ethel knew something was wrong, for her eyes had gone cloudy.

Mrs. Ross had been widowed for four years. Her husband, Tom Ross, had once been a prospector, friend to Freddie Waite. He had been in on the Holcomb Valley gold strike back in '59, made some good money before his vein ran out. Unlike many others, he had kept most of his money, made a few good investments. Then the desert captured him on a trip to the Anza-Borrego, and he began prospecting again. He built a home in Ramona, bought a mule and went into the desert for weeks at a time. He built a dry rocker and brought home enough gold to keep him interested. He had helped Freddie learn the fine points of prospecting, but had not lived long enough to see Waite find a rich claim. One day he got bit by a rattlesnake, ironically, as he was on the way home, and had died in agony a day later. Since then, Ethel had lived off her husband's investments and savings. Now, she took care of Bobbie.

"About time for bed, Bobbie," said Lorelei.

"Do I have to?"

"Yes, I think so. I have to leave soon."

"Where you goin'? To see Gran-pa?"

"No. To San Diego."

"I go San Diego."

She took the boy in her arms, hugged him. She kissed him, tears brimming her eyes. Ethel put down her knitting.

"I'll help tuck him in," she said.

"Thank you, Ethel."

Lorelei knew it was important that Ethel do this.

That way Bobbie did not miss her so. They took the boy to his bedroom, hugged him until he was satisfied, kissed him goodnight. Ethel closed the door quietly. Lorelei dabbed at her eyes.

"I've made some tea," said Ethel. "We can talk in the kitchen."

The kitchen was large, festooned with copper ladles, iron pots, skillets, potted flowers, colorful decorations on the walls. The widow spent a lot of time there. The table was sturdy, square, with a flowered tablecloth hand-sewn by Mrs. Ross.

"Bossie had twins, you said." Lorelei drew herself up, blinked away the last of her tears.

"Yes, a heifer and a bull."

"Is it true that the female will be sterile?"

"It's true. Freemartin. That's what they call it."

"I wish I was sterile."

"Hush, child. Don't talk that way."

"Every time I look at Bobbie, it all comes back. The hate."

"You shouldn't. Not with Bobbie. He's a good boy."

"I know he is, Ethel."

"He's got your eyes."

"His blood."

"No! The boy can't help what he is, where he came from. He doesn't know!"

Ethel picked up the teakettle with a furious gesture, poured the steaming water into cups. Loose tea leaves floated, steeped. She lifted the saucers, brought them to the table. Her eyes were flashing, yet she kept her voice low so that Bobbie wouldn't hear. She put her hand on Lorelei's.

Lorelei stared at her, beyond her.

"Child, you have to look to the future," said the widow. "The boy needs you. He—he needs . . ."

"A father," said Lorelei bitterly.

"Someday. But now he needs you, Freddie."

"Freddie's dead."

Ethel reared back in her chair, gasped. Her face flushed with color. Her hand trembled. Steam rose from the teacups, the vapor wafting away with their breathing.

Lorelei told her the whole story, mentioning Gunn, but holding back on her feelings for the man.

Ethel listened intently.

"There was a Gunn once up on Grasshopper Creek when Pa Ross was alive, working the gold fields in Alder Gulch, up Virginny City way. Montana Territory. He was quite a young man."

Lorelei's interest perked.

"Could it be the same man?"

"I don't know. He had pale blue eyes that were like steel and he was an honest man. We heard he was an outlaw, though. Much later."

Lorelei trembled.

"Ethel, I—I'm confused. I don't know this man. He—he was hurt and I wanted to comfort him, but I'm afraid. Afraid he'll hurt me or leave me."

"Drink your tea, Lorelei. We'll talk a spell."

Ethel calmed down, so did Lorelei. The two women sipped their tea, relaxed. After a time, Ethel began speaking.

"I know how you feel about your father, child. And about the man who killed him. But vengeance is not yours to mete out. Stay here with me and Bobbie. We'll make a home here for you."

"I—I can't. Don't you see? My father wanted that mine. He claimed it. I can't just let them take it away from him."

"They might anyway. You could get killed."

"I can't think about that."

"Then think about Bobbie."

Lorelei fell silent. She fought back tears. In her heart she knew Ethel was right, but she couldn't just give up. Snake and Chigger would count on that. If someone didn't stop them, they'd take everything they wanted. Everything.

Lorelei got up.

"I'm going now, Ethel. Take care of Bobbie for me. No matter what happens. Do you need any more money?"

"No. Please don't do this, Lorelei."

"My mind's made up. I—I'll see you soon, I hope. Tell Bobbie . . ."

"Yes?"

"Tell Bobbie I love him."

El Monterrey was crowded. Painted women fanned themselves in the heat. A Mexican noodled on a guitar, picking out chords, snatches of melody, in a corner. Men lined the bar, their shirts open to their waists, or wore only sweat-stained undershirts. A lone bartender tried hard to keep up with the orders as men shouted at him, laughed at his predicament.

Gunn stood in the doorway leading from the hotel, scanned the room. He saw no faces he recognized. He strode to the bar. A woman got up, approached him, turned away when she looked at his eyes, the hard lines of his face. Men looked at him as he passed by, shrugged.

A grizzled prospector, alone at a table, stood up, doffed his hat.

"Come and set, stranger," he said. "It's summer and the darkies are gay."

Gunn laughed in spite of himself.

The Mexican started to play "My Old Kentucky Home."

"I'm Buzzard Anderson and I'm mean as a polecat," said the prospector, "but I'll buy you a drink from my bottle, stranger, and that cuts out a twenty-minute wait for old Pedro there."

Gunn angled toward the table.

"Obliged," he said, looking Anderson over.

The man sat like a hickory stump, but there was little fat on him. He was short, stocky, sinewed like a fighting bull. He wore a beard that matched his bushy, overhanging eyebrows and his eyes glinted like gold flecks in quartz. His hat was dusty, but it had once been coal black. His clothes were tight-fitting, worn to a comfortable condition.

"Set," said Anderson.

Gunn sat down, looking around the saloon once more. There were a lot of windows and all of them were open to let out the heat. They let the heat in and the room was like a sweatbath.

"Good poison here," said Buzzard, shoving the bottle toward Gunn. Then, under his breath, he said, "If you be a man named Gunn, they's coyotes sniffing your trail."

"I'm Gunn."

Anderson laughed heartily, slapped Gunn on the

back. He cracked his face open with a snaggle-toothed grin and acted as though all was well.

"I brung two glasses just in case I met a like-minded soul. The desert's hot and the gold stays hid. The mules balk and the water holes fill up with sand, but a man can live out there in bliss, my friend, and even the Gilas and snakes don't bother no big desert rat like Buzzard. I eat snakes and lizards and other creatures."

This he said in a loud voice and the curious in the room went back to their interrupted conversations so that the prospector could tell Gunn what he had to say.

"You got two on your tail, Gunn," he said, sotto voce, "and they're lookin' mighty hard."

"One of 'em hurt?"

"The big one, Kimmons. Torres, he's like summer lightning, like a whip you don't see till it tickles your balls."

"I know 'em."

"You know hell, then, and if you're a hardcase you don't fidget none."

"I'm really looking for two other men."

"Oh?"

"Snake and Chigger."

Anderson's countenance flickered. His eyes glistened with recognition.

"Two of the worst. And they was through here yestiddy."

"Left already?"

Anderson shrugged.

"They saw who they come to see."

Gunn leaned forward, interested.

"Who was that?" he asked.

Buzzard leaned back in his chair.

118

"Pour your drink, Gunn, and listen careful."

Gunn took the empty glass, poured whiskey into it. Something scratched against the back of his neck. Something clawed there. He looked around the room, at the open windows. He saw only darkness outside. The people in the saloon paid them no attention.

"Drink," said Buzzard, lifting his own glass.

Gunn drank. The whiskey was powerful, strong. But it was better than tanglefoot. He tasted no hot peppers or tobacco. No licorice.

"You can see, eh?"

Gunn's eyebrows arched.

"Reason you're still alive, I reckon."

"Huh?"

"There's a half dozen men in this room who would have left right now, run straight to Kimmons if they'd knowed who you was."

"I don't understand."

"Torres and Kimmons said they was lookin' for a blind man. I reckon that was you. I recognized you right off, though. Seed you before, a few years back. Up on Grasshopper Creek. You ain't as lean, but your eyes is the same. Like silver coins sometimes when the light hits 'em right. Yessir, it's been a long time. The Widow Ross 'members you, too, and if you need some friends here in Ramona you got 'em."

Gunn thought about what Anderson had said.

A long time ago.

A man didn't know when he had friends or where he might find them.

"I guess I owe you something," said Gunn.

"Nope. I owe you something. Those were my pals up there you helped out. All of us, really. Listen, I got something important to tell you. Not only about Torres and Kimmons, but about this here Snake and Chigro you're chasin'."

A man nearby, straining to hear, drew back, scraped his chair getting up. Gunn looked at him. So did Anderson.

"Uh oh," said Buzzard, "looks like we done been eavesdropped."

"I'd like to hear what you have to say. If you think it would help."

The man left the saloon and Gunn thought no more about him. He took another drink, hunched over the table.

Buzzard began to talk.

CHAPTER THIRTEEN

Lorelei knocked on the door.

"Gunn?"

She tapped again. The door swung open. Puzzled, she peered into the darkness of the room. The hotel room should have been locked. Gunn should have been there.

"Are you there? Gunn?"

No answer.

She went inside, holding her breath.

Her skin went prickly. She found her way to the lamp, fumbled for the matches. She struck one on the sparker, lifted the glass chimney. The wick caught and light spread from the lamp.

Gunn was not there.

But someone had been there.

His saddlebags and hers were strewn over the floor, the contents scattered like cast-off junk. A piece of paper lay on the table. She lifted the lamp, carried it over to the table. She picked up the piece of paper.

The handwriting was crude, but the message was clear.

"KEEP YOUR MOUTH SHUT OR DIE," the note said.

Lorelei trembled. The paper rattled in her hand.

"Gunn . . ." she murmured, suddenly afraid.

Was he dead? Was the note meant for him or for her? Or for both of them?

Where was he?

Lorelei opened her purse, checked her pistol.

She looked around the room. The rifles were there. Nothing had been taken. But she felt defiled, invaded. Whoever had been there had just walked right in, looked through their things. Like thieves. Like masked, faceless bandits. Her skin grew clammy with sweat. She gritted her teeth, suddenly angry.

Who could have come here?

Kimmons? Torres?

Or Snake and Chigger?

She felt ransacked herself. Raped.

She had to find Gunn. If he was still alive. But he was blind. He would have been helpless if someone had come up. She looked for blood, for signs of a struggle. Something caught her eye.

The bandage Doc Gold had put around his head!

She picked it up, weighed it in her hand.

It told her nothing.

Whoever had violated their room could have taken the bandage off Gunn's eyes.

Or Gunn could have.

She felt suffocated in the room. The door was open. From downstairs she could hear the sound of laughter, talk, music from a guitar.

It was a place to start, to look for Gunn.

She blew out the lamp, walked to the door. She left her purse open, so she could reach her pistol. She would find Gunn, dead or alive. She prayed that he was alive, but her heart sank, even so. A blind man had no chance against those who were after them, who left the warning note.

A blind man in Ramona was as good as dead.

"I have no proof, you understand," said Buzzard, "only suspicions, same as Freddie Waite, a pal of mine, but you see a lot in the desert and you see a lot in town."

"Freddie's dead," said Gunn. "You didn't know?"

Anderson paled visibly beneath his brushy beard. His eyes faded as if a shadow had passed over his face.

"Freddie? You sure?"

"I saw him killed." Gunn told him about Snake and Chigger, what they had done.

Buzzard drank four fingers of whiskey while Gunn talked and the minutes ticked by. Gunn's neck began to tighten up as if something was knotting up the muscles. And something still crawled back there. He looked at the dark windows, at the crowd, but he saw nothing unusual. He seemed to be accepted by the crowd and the crowd seemed bent on its own alcoholic destruction. The Mexican played fragments of songs as if he was listening to the talk and trying to play music that would fit in. There was no beginning to the tunes, no end. He just played a wide variety of gringo and Mexican melodies that were familiar, but not complete. It was both annoying and soothing. Annoying because he never finished anything, and he never started at the beginning.

"God, poor Freddie. He and I were like brothers, I reckon, though we seldom saw much of one another. I heard he hit a good strike and good friends don't horn in, only wait until they's invited. He must have put up a good fight."

"He did."

"That Snake, he's dangerous, and Chigger's like dynamite all capped, fused and lit. Liable to go off any time."

"You were going to tell me something—something that would help."

"As the Christ is holy, Gunn, it done slipped my ever-lovin' mind what I was goin' to say. Freddie being six feet under and all."

"Buzzard," said Gunn evenly, "I made Freddie a promise. I said I'd get those men. If you have any information, I sure as hell plumb promise my horse and saddle to get it out of you."

Anderson reached for the bottle. Gunn grasped his wrist, squeezed it tightly.

"Not yet," he said. "Think. Tell me what you know."

Buzzard withdrew his hand. Gunn let it slip away. His eyes held steady on Anderson's, pale gray-blue eyes that were like the bottom parts of pewter spoons.

"Mister, they'd kill me for tellin' you."

"Who?"

"Tricky, ain't ye?"

"I stick to a thing."

"Yeah, you do. All right. But lean close and you leave me out of it."

"Done." Gunn leaned forward. So did Buzzard.

Anderson opened his mouth. Started to say a word.

"Ol . . ."

An explosion blasted the rest of what Buzzard meant to say into a deafening roar. An orange flame blossomed at a window. A hole appeared in Buzzard's neck. Blood gushed out. His neck snapped with the impact. The ball shattered the spine. Buzzard fell to the floor, twitching spasmodically. Gunn shoved his chair back, drew his pistol.

Women screamed.

Smoke hung in the empty window.

Men dove for the floor.

At the hotel entrance, Lorelei stood, frozen, a hand over her mouth.

Gunn raced to the window, looked out into the darkness. He heard the sound of running feet. He saw no one.

The shingle outside the adobe read: "ANTHONY SMITHERS, Attorney at Law." The office was among a number of similar buildings on a hill overlooking the Pacific Ocean in San Diego. Palm trees shaded the hitchrail.

Gunn dismounted, took Lorelei's reins. She was still shattered over the killing of Buzzard Anderson the night before. That and the note had driven her to the point of hysteria. Gunn had calmed her down, gotten her to the room, but they had left shortly afterwards, riding out of Ramona in the dark.

Now, weary and dusty, they looked at each other with red-rimmed eyes.

"This the place?"

"Yes," she said tightly. "Smithers is our attorney."

Gunn snugged her reins to the hitchrail, helped her up the loose steps. The sea air had turned the wood gray, warped it. The porch sagged. Lorelei went in without knocking. Gunn followed. The morning had not gone well. They had learned the worst at the claim office a half hour ago.

He had asked her about the syllable on Anderson's lips when he had been shot. She could not figure out what he had meant to say. "Ol" could mean anything. He had told her to think. Of a first name, a last name, anything that began with those letters.

Nothing.

But someone had followed them out of Ramona. When the sun came up he had seen dust behind them. Later he had backtracked, found the hoof marks of two horses. But the men had eluded him and once they came over the hill and down into San Diego through lush trees and cool shade, he had seen their pursuers no more.

The anteroom was furnished with wicker and woven chairs. Small Indian blankets adorned the bare adobe walls, along with faded gauche paintings of the sea and the hills of San Diego. A man coughed in the next room.

"Tony? It's Lorelei."

Anthony Smithers was a small, nervous man in his late twenties. His hair was slicked down. He wore a white suit and a dark tie that was slightly askew. His hands were delicate, expressive, moved when he talked. He appeared in the doorway, a pipe in his hand.

"Lorelei! Come in, come in. And you're Mister . . . ?"

"Gunn. Just Gunn."

"Quiet this morning. A case this afternoon. My

clerk's out to lunch early. You look tired, Lorrie. Sit down, Gunn. What's on your mind?"

Smithers' desk was stacked with lawbooks, papers, pads, pencils. Books lined his bookcase behind him and along one wall. His law degree was framed, tacked into the adobe. It hung slightly askew. A breeze blew through the one window and palm leaves rattled pleasantly. The furniture was solid, a big desk, wide oak chairs, a sleeping couch against the other wall. The room smelled of sweet pipe tobacco and apples.

"We've just come from the claim office," she said as she sat down.

"Freddie send you in?"

"Freddie's dead."

Smithers leaned forward in his swivel chair.

"I—I don't understand," he said, his eyes blinking nervously. He slid the pipe around in his hands. The bowl was empty.

Lorelei told him everything that had happened, including Gunn's witnessing her father's murder, the death of Anderson, and the fact that someone was following them.

"I see," said Smithers, who began to fill his pipe from a wooden canister on his desk. He tamped the tobacco down, struck a match. He sucked airily on the stem, drawing flame through the bowl.

Lorelei brought out a copy of the claim.

"This the new one?" asked the attorney.

"Yes. I had a copy made."

"Interesting," said Smithers, looking it over. "You say Snake and Chigger killed your father. And you think they filed a claim on the mine."

"Yes, according to Gunn. The claim was filed late

127

yesterday as you can see."

"You know who this is?" asked Smithers, pointing to the name on the document.

"No," said Lorelei.

Gunn watched as Smithers twirled in his chair, worried the pipe around in his mouth. The air overhead became wreathed in smoke. The attorney looked at the paper, put it down, picked it up again. The pipe-stem clicked against his teeth.

He got up, went to a file cabinet, opened it. He brought out a sheaf of papers in a manila folder. The label on the folder read "WAITE." He sat down, looked through them, checked the new document again. Lorelei looked at Gunn, her eyebrows rising as if she was exasperated or trying to explain Smithers' slowness to him.

"Well, well, well," said Smithers. "Very interesting. I have two claims of your father's here. And his will. And some other pertinent depositions regarding the claims. And this new claim made out to one C.O. Molinero of Julian. It appears that Molinero's claim overlaps one of yours."

"I know," said Lorelei. "Gunn went over the claims, gave me the figures."

"May I see those?"

Lorelei took them out of her satchel, handed them to Smithers. Smithers puffed and checked figures. The breeze blew the smoke around the room, pulled wisps of it outside.

"Looks to me like Freddie wanted to take out another twenty acres," said Smithers. "Put it in your name, Lorelei. I can file this today if you like."

"What about this other one? Molinero's?"

"Might be disputed. Probably will. There are a number of new claims under that name."

"There are?"

"Seems so. My clerk automatically checks mining claims once a week. I don't know who Molinero is, but he is buying them up or staking them pretty regularly."

"Can he do that?" asked Gunn.

"Oh, yes. He has to work them, that's all. Show proof. They're widely spread out. This one is very interesting, though."

"You keep saying that," said Gunn. "What do you mean?"

"Well, in the others, he has shown bills of sale, put them in a corporation. This appears to be a staked claim. A personal claim."

"So?"

"So, we have a dispute. Lorelei's father claimed one mine, the other was not yet filed. I was waiting for him to come in with the measurements. Since you have them, I'll file. But it appears there will be an overlapping. You mark the claims correctly?"

"I did," said Gunn.

"Well, we'll give it a try. Still, most interesting." Smithers removed his pipe, looked directly at Gunn.

"Damnit, Tony, quit saying that," said Lorelei. "What's interesting about it?"

"Oh, the whole business is interesting, but I was thinking about Gunn here. Are you staying in town? Where will you be?"

"We'll stay as long as necessary," said Lorelei. "At the Cortez, I imagine."

"Good place. I should have some information for you by tomorrow."

Smithers stood up, offered his hand to Gunn. Gunn shook it. The man was still staring at him oddly.

Lorelei smiled weakly.

"Is that all?" she said.

Smithers smiled.

"Oh, the interesting thing about Gunn here is that I saw a poster just this morning that resembles him slightly."

"A poster?" asked Lorelei.

"Yes. It seems he is wanted for murder. There is a reward of five hundred dollars for him."

"For Gunn?"

"Yes. Dead or alive."

CHAPTER FOURTEEN

The Cortez was a two-story hotel at the center of town, set like a hub in the center of a wheel. San Diego was busy, the streets clogged with wagons. Indians, Mexicans, Americans flooded the thoroughfares, all seemingly in a hurry to do business while the sun was shining. Vendors hawked their wares at every corner. Indians carried bundles of goods on their backs. Fishermen pushed carts through the streets and women displayed their blankets and pottery under shaded awnings made of thatched palm leaves. There was an excitement in the air and a bustle that contrasted with the sleepy atmosphere of Julian and Ramona.

A church bell rang the hour. Seagulls and pigeons fluttered in shimmering waves as they rode through the plaza. Sleepy, sombreroed men dozed against the buildings and benches; a clutch of youngsters chased a squirrel across the square.

Gunn saw his picture tacked to a post that held up the porch roof of the Hotel El Cortez. He ripped it off, looked at it closely.

131

"Where did these come from?" asked Lorelei.

"Ink's fresh, but the information isn't. Someone did some checking."

"I don't understand."

The poster read: "William Gunnison, alias 'GUNN,' WANTED for MURDER. $500 Reward. Dead or Alive. Contact any U.S. Marshal."

"I'm wanted in Wyoming. It's a trumped-up charge. Someone heard about it, had these printed up. I doubt if the marshal here knows a damned thing about it."

"You mean these are just posters? They're not official."

"No," said Gunn, a slight grin flickering over his lips.

"But how can you be sure? That drawing looks somewhat like you."

Gunn crumpled up the poster, tossed it into the street. A passing burro mashed it into the dust.

"Because," said Gunn, going up the steps to the hotel doors, "the reward is too cheap."

"What?" exclaimed Lorelei, mystified by his attitude.

"Went up to a thousand a long time back," he said, disappearing through the doors.

He kept his hat brim low, checked them into the hotel. He didn't use his own name, but signed them in as G. Waite and L. Waite. If someone was riding drag on them, they'd take the bait.

"I want another room for a friend who'll be right behind us," said Gunn in Spanish. "Want it right across the hall."

The Mexican clerk nodded.

Gunn signed a fictitious name: Jed Randall.

Lorelei started to say something. Gunn put a finger

132

to his lips.

"We'll keep his key," said Gunn.

He laid out the money for the rooms, took Lorelei upstairs.

"Who . . . ?"

"Jed was a friend of mine. Died up in Oro City. Died bad. Used his name for a reason."

Gunn went to the room registered under the name of Randall. It was directly opposite the one registered to the Waites. With the door open slightly, he had a good view of the other door. He opened that, too, left it slightly ajar.

Inside the Randall room, Lorelei sighed, sat on the bed.

"Everything's happening so fast. Maybe you'd better explain what you're doing."

Gunn sprawled in a straight chair, weariness weighting his bones.

"I figure Kimmons and Torres are breathing down our backs. Shouldn't take them long to find us. They'll check the hotel register, come after us. I'll be here, ready for them."

"You'll kill them?"

"Depends."

"On what?"

"On how they behave when they walk into that room over there."

Lorelei shuddered.

"In cold blood?"

"No. They'll have a chance. They probably left that note for you. I take that as a serious threat."

"Yes," admitted Lorelei. She lay back on the bed, closed her eyes. Gunn watched her, touched a hand to

133

his forehead. The bruise was healing up. His own eyes were tired, but he could see. The ringing and buzzing in his ears had stopped. The headaches came less frequently and were less severe.

He tried to sort out all the scraps fluttering around his mind. C.O. Molinero. A new name. Unfamiliar to him. But, whoever Molinero was, he was serious. Dead serious. It was certain that Snake and Chigger worked for him. Probably Kimmons and Torres as well. And others. Working claims that must be paying off for a man to go so far as to kill Freddie Waite and file on his property. But Molinero was smart, too. Stayed in the background. Let others do his dirty work. Snake and Chigger. Kimmons and Torres.

And another.

The man Snake and Chigger had picked up in their flight to San Diego.

John Smith.

An alias, most likely.

But another figure in the puzzle.

Suddenly, it occurred to Gunn that he might not be facing just two men, Kimmons and Torres, but four or five. Snake and Chigger might still be in town, waiting for Kimmons. This "John Smith" could be with them. If so, then they would be outgunned. He couldn't ask Lorelei to back him in his bold play. He hoped to take Kimmons and Torres out without bloodshed. Just get the drop on them, lock them up for a while and keep them out of his hair. But he could only plan so far. He didn't know what kind of a hold Molinero had on them, but it must be pretty strong for them to keep tracking him. And Snake knew who he was. The fliers proved that. Crude as they were, the wanted posters implied that this bunch knew the law in San Diego, could get such information from the sheriff or marshal.

Lorelei startled him.

"I thought of a name," she said, breaking into the silence.

"Huh?" Gunn was lost.

"What Buzzard said when he died. Or tried to say."

Gunn drew up to full attention. He had almost forgotten about that small scrap.

"Go on, tell me," he said.

"Well, it may not mean anything, but I've been running that syllable through my mind. Trying to think of all the people it might fit. It's odd, but I can only think of two names that begin like that. Ollie and Oliver."

"How about Oliphant, Olive?"

"All right. But there's an Oliver Miller who owns the mercantile store in Julian."

"Sure?"

"Yes. Julian Mercantile. That's why I couldn't fit the name before. And Oliver is such a pipsqueak. I don't see how he could be connected to any of this."

"No, well, I'd like to talk to him, anyway."

"Maybe Emma would be able to tell us what her husband meant."

"Emma?"

"Why, Emma Anderson, Buzzard's wife."

"First I've heard of it. I gathered a man like Buzzard was a bachelor. A loner."

Lorelei sat up on the bed, laughed.

"Why, Buzzard's always been married. His first wife died and he married Emma right off. Has a daughter by his first wife, Amanda."

"How could he support two women?"

"Buzzard did well. He just never showed his money much. Gave it all to Mandy and Emma."

Gunn's respect and admiration for Buzzard rose several notches. It was too bad he had been killed. He might have been able to clear this whole mess up. Gunn felt guilty about that. Buzzard had been the one to warn him when others in Ramona had kept quiet. He had stuck his neck out a country mile and gotten his head lopped off. A man like that was seldom encountered.

"Looks like I'll have to pay his widow and daughter a visit," said Gunn.

"You stay clear of Emma Anderson," said Lorelei sharply. "Why she's not much older than Mandy. And, she's very rich."

"Lorelei," teased Gunn, "you sound almost jealous."

Her eyes flashed and Gunn's grin died on his face.

He had touched a nerve. Glimpsed another side of Lorelei.

There was no end to the woman. No end at all.

The two men walked into the Hotel El Cortez just at dusk.

There was another clerk on duty.

One of the men entering the hotel limped.

The other was a Mexican.

"We'll take a look at your register," said Kimmons. "Looking for a friend."

The clerk, a Mexican, opened the book, turned it around to face Kimmons. Torres, standing half a foot behind Kimmons, speared the clerk with a look. The clerk went back to his desk, sat down. He ignored the two men.

"There," said Kimmons, "fifth name up. That's them."

He failed to see the name underneath. But, then, it wouldn't have meant anything to him. The signatures were different and he didn't notice.

Torres looked, nodded.

"Pretty bold, ain't they?" grinned Kimmons.

Torres said nothing.

"Well, let's get to it. Clerk, you stay put. I want to see you right where you are when we come back down. Savvy?"

The clerk nodded, shrank into the shadows. The lamp on the desk seemed to match his trembling.

Kimmons and Torres made little sound as they climbed the stairs. The hallway was lit by dim lamps. The two men found their way to the door they sought. It was open, slightly. The room was dark.

Kimmons gestured. Torres frowned.

"That's it," whispered the limping man.

"Too quiet," said Torres.

Kimmons grinned.

Their footsteps creaked on the floor as they took up positions on either side of the door.

Inside the room opposite, Gunn heard the stealthy sounds. He tiptoed to the door, drew his pistol. Lorelei drew in a breath, held it.

"Is it . . . ?"

"Shhh," said Gunn.

A quiet settled.

There was a waiting while men breathed and thought. A waiting when men thought about death and

137

killing. A waiting while the silence weighed itself on scales and the tipping was like a clock that made no sound, but only moved like a hammer beat in the heart. And the heart pumped like a lung and breathed like the empty air through a gun barrel after the hammer is cocked.

Kimmons shot a glance at Torres.

Torres bowed his head in an assenting nod.

The two men drew pistols.

Gunn opened his door a crack.

He looked at the Mexican's ear, waited for it to twitch.

Torres leaned into the dark opening like a puma about to pounce. He seemed like a whip about to crackle and flick.

Kimmons edged toward the dark opening of the door.

He looked at Torres, stormed inside the room. Torres raced after him.

The door swung wide, inside the room.

Gunn moved, darting across the hall. He hugged the wall, took a breath. He cocked his pistol, stepped inside.

"He ain't here!" said Kimmons.

"Cabron!" exclaimed Torres.

Gunn slid along the inside wall, out of the light. He made no sound.

"Kimmons, drop it," he said.

Torres whirled, his pistol bucking in his hand. Explosions rocked the room. Torres fired at the door. "You sonofabitch!" said Kimmons, spotting Gunn, taking deadly aim with his pistol.

Gunn bent to a crouch, squeezed the trigger.

Torres swung his pistol to take aim on Gunn.

The .45 Colt in Gunn's hand twitched as flame spouted from the barrel, as the powder exploded. Torres shivered as the lead ball thunked into his gut. His eyes glazed with hatred and pain.

Kimmons started to squeeze the trigger.

Gunn fingered his Colt, felt the reassuring nudge of the grip as it bucked with life. Kimmons walked right into the slug. The bullet tore a hole low in the right side of his chest. He shuddered, fired.

The heat of the burning powder scorched Gunn's face, but the ball plunked into the wall six inches over his head. Kimmons tried to keep walking toward Gunn, bring his pistol up to fire again.

Torres stood there, swaying. His pistol barked again and the ball ripped a slice into the wood floor, stinging Gunn's legs with splinters. Gunn shot him in the right lung.

Torres melted to the floor, mortally wounded.

Kimmons kept coming on.

Gunn shot his leg out from under him. The big man fell to the floor with a wheeze.

Torres rolled over on his back, stared up at the ceiling.

Kimmons started to crawl toward Gunn.

Wouldn't the man quit?

"Give it up, Kimmons," said the tall, gray-eyed man.

"Bastard," said Kimmons through clenched teeth.

He raised his pistol.

Gunn shot him in the face.

Kimmons' nose exploded like an overripe tomato, showering blood in all directions. The back of his head blew away like a pie plate. Brain matter flocked the walls like soggy wads of cotton.

Torres swore in Spanish.

Gunn crawled to him, straddled the Mexican.

Blood bubbled from the wounded man's mouth, streamed from the corners of his lips.

"You ain't got much time," said Gunn. "Tell me where I can find Molinero."

A light flickered in the Mexican's eyes. A dim light that quickly passed. He opened his mouth to laugh. He grinned with bloodstained teeth.

His lips moved.

He said two words. In English.

Torres quivered one last time and his eyes closed. Forever.

Gunn stood up, blew out the acrid stench of black powder from his nostrils. The room reeked of sour gunpowder and death.

"Fuck you, too, Torres," said Gunn, striding toward the door.

CHAPTER FIFTEEN

Lorelei's face was a chalk mask.

"Did you . . . did they . . . ?" she stammered.

"Yes. They're both dead."

"And you?" There was tenderness in her voice.

"Sound. We have to leave. Now. I do, anyway."

"Yes. Yes, of course. Where?"

"Away from here. Someplace safe. If there is such a place."

Lorelei began hefting her saddlebags, satchel. Gunn reloaded his pistol, threw his saddlebags over his shoulder. They walked down the hall, Gunn in the lead. Lorelei looked back once at the room across the hall and shuddered.

"That could have been us in there," she said softly.

"Yes."

The clerk stood back in the shadows. Gunn tossed the keys on the desk.

"Oh, it is you," said the frightened man. "I thought . . ."

"You thought wrong," said Gunn.

141

People stared at them, but no one tried to stop them. Earlier, they had stripped their horses at the Downtown Livery. They headed there now as darkness settled over the city. A few lamps were lit and the vendors were all gone. A man passed by.

"What was all the shooting about?" he asked.

"I didn't hear any shooting," said Gunn.

"Damned Chinks and their fireworks." The man muttered something else and went on his way. Lorelei suppressed a laugh. Hysteria bubbled just below the surface.

"Those men . . . did they say anything about . . . Snake?"

"I didn't ask," said Gunn.

Gunn and Lorelei found a rooming house in El Cajon where they didn't ask questions. They had a late supper after graining the horses, rubbing them down. Gunn was sure that they hadn't been followed, but he had seen more than one flier tacked to buildings in San Diego. Here, in a lonely gorge, away from the sea, they might be safe for a while.

"I want you," said Lorelei, after supper.

Gunn stood in the shadows, smoking. She sat on the porch in a rocking chair.

"It doesn't make sense," he said.

"What?"

"You. Me."

"Don't you like me anymore?"

He dragged deep on the cigarette. The tip glowed like an angry eye.

"I don't understand a woman like you. You change

142

so fast."

"I—I can't help it."

"Sometimes I think you don't like men at all."

"I like you, Gunn."

"Not all the time."

"No. I'm afraid of you, too."

Gunn put out his cigarette, leaned over the porch, looked up at her.

"Afraid of me?"

"Afraid of what you do to me. The hold you have on me."

"I didn't notice it," he said sarcastically.

"You ought to. You notice a lot. You know where to touch me, how to hold me. Maybe you know too much. About some things."

"You talk in riddles, Lorelei."

She sighed, got up from the chair.

"When I look at you sometimes I get hot all over and then cold. Right now, I'm steaming inside. Empty. I want you to fill me."

He laughed harshly.

"I think you've put your finger on it," he said.

"What?"

"You take me when you want me—shove me aside when you're through."

"Why, Gunn, I believe you're pouting. You're hurt."

"Get inside," he said gruffly.

She purred when he touched her.

Lamplight burnished her naked body to a coppery glow.

God, he ached for her! She was so damned beautiful,

143

so damned loving, he felt his insides churn with lust. She had a hold on him and he was beginning to hate it. She knew a lot, herself. She knew what to do with a man, yet she had that reserve, that mystery he couldn't penetrate. Something inside her that was secret. And powerful.

He looked at the dark thatch between her legs.

His hand stroked the fine hairs until they raised up, electrified.

Lorelei shivered all over.

"Oh, what you're doing to me," she sighed.

He had kissed her until her neck and face were strawberry. He had played with her until she writhed and squirmed with desire. Yet she hadn't invited him to couple with her. Not yet. He leaned over now and kissed her breast. The nipple was hard, rubbery. He slid his tongue over the uneven surface, coiled around the base.

"Yes," she purred. "So nice."

"Damnit, Lorelei, it's late."

"Don't be in a hurry."

Something was bothering her. She wanted him, but she was holding back. He couldn't figure it out. Another one of her mysteries. She touched him now, squeezing his cock with firm fingers. A shoot of desire coursed through his loins. He nuzzled the other breast, sprawled over her body. She drew him to her, but did not spread her legs.

He took her head in his hands, kissed her earlobes. He caressed the back of her neck, extended his fingers through her hair, massaged her scalp. She twisted, arched her back. She moaned.

His penis seeped the clear fluids. She dabbed the

144

crown with her finger tip, smearing the liquid. His cock throbbed, pulsed with the fresh engorgement of blood.

Suddenly, she released him, pushed him away.

Dumbfounded, Gunn looked at her.

"I have to ask you something," she said.

"It must be mighty important."

"If we stopped now, would you be disappointed?" Her lips were damp, clung tightly to her teeth.

"Yes."

"Would you not touch me any more if I asked you not to."

"If that's what you wanted. Lorelei . . . don't play games with me."

"Wait."

"All right."

"I have to know this. I have to!"

"Go on. What?"

"Would you rape me if I refused you any more liberties?"

He propped himself up on an elbow. His eyes slits of confusion.

"What kind of a question is that?"

"Please. I have to know. Would you rape me?"

"No."

Lorelei let out a breath that was like a sigh of relief. She looked up at him, tried to bore through his eyes. Her mouth drew up as if she was struggling to say the right words. The words she meant to say.

"No matter what?"

"Lorelei, this is stupid. This kind of talk. You're playing with fire. I don't know what I'd do. But . . ."

"But what?"

"There's no reason to rape you. Is there? You want

145

me. I want you. Isn't that the way it should be between a man and a woman?"

She put a hand on his chest, threaded her fingers through the matted hair. He felt like slapping her. Or choking her. He felt his hardness diminish. She was killing the moment. Killing his desire with her talk, her strange questions.

"Yes," she breathed. "It should be that way. But some men . . . Gunn, did you ever rape a woman?"

"No."

"Never?"

"Never, damnit. Lorelei, what's the point?"

She slid against him.

"Hold me," she whispered. "Hold me tight. And gentle."

His mind rebelled against her request. But her body was warm and pliant and he ached for her. His hardness returned. Instantly.

She kissed him on the lips. Smothered him. Probed his mouth with her tongue. Her hands were restless on his flesh, kneading him, clutching him, scarring him temporarily with their heat, their urgency. She pressed her loins into his, rubbed his rock-hard cock with her sex-cleft. Rubbed him up and down, generating fresh heat so that his senses reeled, his desire grew into an urgent pressure of will.

He tugged her to him, wrestled with her. Her mouth hung open and he stabbed it with his tongue. He ground his hips against hers, wanting to open the portal with his key, to spread her legs and push on in to the honey like some sniffing, hungry animal. He didn't care about her feelings, her games, only about satisfaction, gratification.

146

And Lorelei knew it.

He knew that she knew it.

"Damn you," he growled. "Spread your legs."

She locked her legs tight.

"Don't tease me, woman."

She drew away from him and her fingernails raked his shoulders. Her mouth popped free of his and her hair fell over her face with the force of her retreat.

"You see?" she rasped. "You'd rape me. You'd pounce on me like a . . ."

"Shut up," he said. "Just shut up."

"I won't! You can't make me, Gunn! You can't make me do anything I don't want to do!"

He saw the madness in her eyes, the hysteria boiling up to the surface of her sanity. He recoiled in shock, horrified by the wildness in her eyes, the clawed shape of her hands. She looked like a cornered cat about to strike out, slash him with furious talons.

Gunn backed off.

He drew a breath, tilted his head upward, closed his eyes. He let out his breath, drew another, letting it even out. He blocked her out of his mind. He thought of peaceful places, calmer times. He thought of high mountain rivers and prairie grasses blowing in the wind. He thought of shady bluffs in Arkansas and green hills that looked like islands in morning mist.

Lorelei's eyes crackled with fear, with hatred.

He slapped her face. Hard.

Her neckbones cracked as her head snapped backwards.

"Steady down, Lorelei," he said. "You're only hurting yourself."

"You bastard," she hissed.

147

"Yes. Because I care about you. I won't take you without your asking. I don't want any woman who doesn't want me. If you want to be raped, go out to the cantinas and paint your face, wear a slitted dress. But don't push me, woman. I don't think being a woman gives you any special privilege. I won't let you prod me or cut off my balls."

He got up from the bed, turned his back on her.

He hated to have slapped her, but he knew she had to be rocked to her senses. Any other man might have taken her head off. Or done what she had been begging for: raped her without mercy. The bitch. She had something in her craw and he hated to see her spoil everything with words that stung and hurt and burrowed deep without any reason behind them.

He was trembling with suppressed rage.

His center, the quiet places of thought, had slipped away. He wasn't angry at her, but at himself, for losing even that much control.

But Lorelei had him. As certain as if he was branded on the haunch, she had him. He wondered if he loved her. Or hated her. It felt as if he was being tested. Tested beyond a man's endurance. He thought of her body, of the loving she had given him, the tenderness. And he thought about what might have turned her sour toward him. He blamed himself.

"Gunn . . ."

There was a catch in her voice. A repressed sob.

He didn't answer.

"I'm sorry. Terribly sorry. I didn't mean it. Any of it. I'm cruel. Hateful. I keep thinking about that man, what he did to me. And what he did to my father. He was the only man I knew and he hurt me. He beat me.

He forced me to . . . to do things. I—I wanted to get over it. I wanted it to be right with some man, with you. But I can't stop thinking of him and I can't keep what he did to me out of my mind."

Gunn turned, looking at her.

She was shrieking, her voice out of control, high-pitched.

"Lorelei," he said softly, "what are you saying?"

"Don't you know?"

"What?"

"About me? What happened? What he did to me?"

"No. I don't know anything. I just know you're a beautiful woman and you're troubled. But I can't reach you. You keep pushing me away. Goading me, sticking your spurs in my flanks."

"Please," she sobbed, "don't rub it in. I—I have been mean and cruel and hateful. Forgive me. I'm just boiling over inside like a teapot on the stove. I hate him so much I—I started to hate you."

He walked back to the bed, stood over her. She looked pitiful. She dabbed at her cheeks, but the tears kept streaking her face. He wanted to lift her up, hold her in his arms, kiss away her fears.

She reached out for him. He took her hand.

"Tell me," he said. "Tell me what he did to you."

"Don't you know? He raped me and I had a baby. Bobbie. Bobbie." She broke into uncontrollable sobs. Her hand shook in his.

"Bobbie? You have a son?"

"Yes, yes, and I can't be a mother to him because I hate his father."

"Who?" Gunn asked.

She sucked in a sobbing breath, stared up at him

149

with red-rimmed eyes.

"Snake," she spat. "Snake Spivey is my son's father and the murderer of my own father!"

Gunn closed his eyes and drifted back to his center, to those mountain rivers and the green hills of Arkansas, the moody bluffs that shadowed his favorite fishing streams.

"Gunn?"

"Yes," he said. "I'm here."

He lay beside her, took her in his arms.

She opened to him like some dark and lovely flower.

CHAPTER SIXTEEN

The two men stood outside the Hotel El Cortez, rifles cradled in their arms, their hips dripping with pistols. They wore shabby, dust-infested clothes that stank of sweat-salt and earth. Their boots were weather-cracked, without polish or oil. Their faces were leather masks burned by sun and wind. They said little and listened much.

Sheriff Gideon Townsend finished his talk with the clerks at the hotel. He strode over to the two men.

"Description fits," he said. "Gunn or Gunnison. You see the fliers?"

One of the men nodded.

"What're you payin'?" asked the taller of the two. He was a lean man in his forties with eyes black as ripe olive pits.

"There's five hunnert on him from Wyoming," said Townsend. "But someone local will sweeten the pot."

"How much?" asked the short man, whose face was hidden by hair.

"At least five hunnert more, mayhap a thousand to boot."

The tall man pursed his lips. His name was Jerry Woolhoyt. His partner was known as Randy Davis. Both men were bounty hunters. They could smell money. They could smell fear and death. Townsend was afraid of them. He had been called to the hotel the night before and had the dead men dragged away. He knew who they were. He had been afraid of them, too. Then someone had come to his office this morning and said that Gunn had killed Kimmons and Torres.

Townsend had been led to believe that someone would rather see Gunn dead and pay for it than to have him brought in alive. This morning, he had taken a poster to the hotel and questioned the clerks to see if Gunn was responsible for the death of the two men killed the previous night. He was satisfied that Gunn had done the deed. The bounty hunters had dogged his tracks all morning, rifles at the ready.

"You got a line on this Gunn?" asked Randy.

"He was tracked here from Ramona, Julian. He lit a shuck after dobe wallin' them two jaspers last night. Might be headed back that way."

"Much obliged, Sheriff," said Woolhoyt. "We'll check around, get back to you."

"You do that."

The bounty hunters walked past the sheriff, went inside the hotel. Townsend swore, strode off toward his horse. It was a hell of a morning. Well, at least someone had left burying money and it wouldn't take all that much to plant two men who didn't have any relatives. He didn't know who was paying for that and putting up the reward, but it didn't matter. Kimmons and Torres were hardcases and the world wouldn't miss them. He hoped he didn't have to track Gunn, though. Just thinking about him made his skin crawl. Kimmons was mean as hell and Torres was even worse. Such men did not die easy or without a fight. Yet a lone man had killed them both and walked away without a scratch, according to the night clerk.

Back at his office, Sheriff Townsend looked through the fliers in his desk drawer. There was nothing on Woolhoyt or Davis. Until two days ago, he had never heard of this man Gunn. Then the envelope had been delivered, with the flier. He looked at it again. It was the one from Wyoming. The one that said, "Wanted Dead or Alive, William Gunnison, alias 'Gunn.'" The reward was for a thousand dollars offered by the Cheyenne town marshal. The charges were murder, escape, and flight to avoid prosecution. Townsend looked at the drawing. There was nothing remarkable about it. Just the eyes. They seemed to stare straight at him. He put the poster back in the bottom of the drawer. He had told Woolhoyt and Davis that the reward was only for five hundred dollars. A mistake, probably, but he could use an extra five hundred. There had been a note inside the envelope with the flier. Offering another five hundred for this Gunn. Fifteen hundred dollars was too much for one saddletramp's life. A murderer, to boot. And, anyway, whoever had the new posters printed up had put down five hundred dollars as the reward. He didn't know who was behind all this sudden interest in a man called Gunn and he didn't want to know.

For now, he just wished Gunn would ride right out of the state and take those two bounty hunters with him.

Gunn kissed her tenderly. He understood a lot more about her since their talk of the night before. Lorelei seemed more calm this morning, less anxious.

"Do you really think it's wise to go back there alone?" she asked.

"It's best we split up. You have to see Smithers and I want to try and pick up this Molinero's trail."

She drew away from him. There was a shyness about her that had not been there in days. As if she had discovered something about herself and him the night before. Their lovemaking had been different, more tender, more relaxed than at previous times. Lorelei had not been the savage, but the willing participant, giving as well as taking.

"You'll see Buzzard's widow?"

"If she'll talk to me. Maybe I can learn something."

"I'm sure," she said, a slight trace of sarcasm coating her words.

"Don't get mean on me, Lorelei. Maybe Emma Anderson can tell me what Buzzard meant to say when he was killed. He had a name. He almost had it out of his mouth."

"Be careful," she said.

"You too."

He kissed her again, picked up his gear. She watched him go through the door without turning around.

"Wait for me in Ramona," she called after him. "I'll be there as soon as I can."

He turned, looked at her. Smiled.

"Hurry," he said quietly.

She felt her insides melt, her knees go soft.

Gunn rode into Ramona late that afternoon.

He had seen no one on his back trail, few people on the road. There had been some farmers, some Mexicans in a buggy pulled by a fine team of horses, a few peons walking north with bundles slung over their shoulders. They had all waved jovially as he rode by and Esquire had eaten up the miles.

In town, the empty hearse passed him by. Stragglers from the cortege did not wave, but spoke quietly among themselves. He doffed his hat to the women, rode out to the cemetery to pay his last respects to Buzzard Anderson.

Outside the cemetery, he passed the preacher who looked up at him with doleful eyes. Gunn rode on, looked for a fresh grave with flowers. He stopped at the picket gate, dismounted. He hitched Esquire to a juniper, strolled into the cemetery.

The two women stood by the open grave, holding onto each other. Men with shovels stood some distance away, smoking, looking up at the sky so that they would not seem to be intruding on the grief of the women. Flowers adorned the gravesite. Gunn thought that Anderson must have had some friends who would miss him now that he was gone.

He took off his hat, stopped a few feet away from the grave. He bowed his head. One of the women looked up at him. They were both dressed in black, carried small black parasols. Their dresses were finely made, were shiny in the late afternoon sun. He could not see their faces through their veils. He stood there, sweat streaking his face, wondering when it would be proper to approach.

One of the women whispered something to the other. A moment later, she slipped her arm free of the other woman, walked his way.

"Did you come for the funeral?" she asked. "If so, I believe you're several moments late."

"No, ma'am," he said, "I came to pay my respects to Mister Anderson and to talk some with his widow."

"And just who are you to intrude at such a mournful time?"

"The name's Gunn, ma'am. I was with Buzz . . . with Mister Anderson when he, ah, died."

The woman swept up her veil, peered closely at Gunn. She was comely, with pale blue eyes, rosy-rimmed from weeping. Her nose was straight, pointed at the end. Her cheeks were slightly chubby and she had a dimple in the center of her chin. A mole next to her mouth was dark and provocative.

"Yes, I heard there was a stranger with my husband when he was killed. A man with a price on his head. An outlaw. And you ran away, did you?"

"No, ma'am."

"I'm Emma Anderson. A widow now. I loved my husband very much. He was odd, but he was kind and considerate. I shall miss him terribly. I question the fact that you did not stay with my husband and perhaps be of help."

"He was dead. I went after his killers."

Emma Anderson drew back in amazement. She reached into her small purse, a clutch bag, and drew out a pair of spectacles. She put them on, regarded Gunn more closely. At the gravesite, the other woman continued to sob quietly, kneeling now in the hot sun, peering into the open grave. Her parasol lay beside her, opened, standing like a silhouette of a miniature wagon wheel.

"So, you went after his killers? Did you know them?" Emma's tone was accusatory, hostile. Gunn stood his ground, shaded his eyes with his hand.

"No. I had an idea who they might be."

Emma snorted, stamped her foot. She seemed about to pounce on Gunn. Instead, she looked over her shoulder toward the woman by the grave.

"Mandy!" she called. "Come here!"

Gunn's heart slid downward in his chest. None of this was going the way he wanted it to. He wanted to offer his condolences, make friends long enough to find out what he needed to know. But, instead, Anderson's widow was ready to claw him to pieces. He sensed the shrouded anger, the veiled killer instinct. Emma looked tough. She would go for the throat—or the balls.

Mandy walked over, twirling her parasol absentmindedly. She lifted her veil and Gunn saw her father's image, a softer one. She was light blond, with pristine blue eyes, deep as a Montana sky, a full mouth, button nose and teeth pretty as polished ivory.

"Yes, Mum," she said. "Is this a friend of Papa's?"

"I'm not quite sure. This is Gunn. The man who was with your father when he was killed. He says he went after the killer."

"Please, ma'am," said Gunn, "I didn't come here to add to your grief or to apologize for my actions. Buzzard went out of his way to offer me help. He was probably killed for talking to me. I take the blame for that. I'm terribly sorry, but what I asked him, just before he was shot, was hellish important. He was about to tell me when . . ."

"When he was shot?" asked Emma.

"Yes."

Mandy, who had said nothing, and who had regarded Gunn curiously, now opened her mouth.

"I know you," she said. "You're Gunn. From Grasshopper Creek."

"I've been there."

Emma looked at her stepdaughter in amazement. Mandy drew in a breath, stepped close.

"Yes," she said. "Emma, I want to talk to you a minute."

"Excuse us, Mister Gunn," said Emma, reacting to Mandy's tug at her arm. The two women walked out of earshot. Mandy began whispering urgently while Gunn waited, wondering what they were talking about. Every so often, the two of them would look at him and then huddle again. He looked toward the gate, at Esquire, at the buggy and horse hitched to a tree some distance beyond. He was tired and he wasn't getting anywhere. He had no remembrance of either Mandy or Buzzard. Grasshopper Creek was a long time ago.

Emma Anderson beckoned to Gunn. Mandy stood straight, stepped slightly to one side.

"Mister Gunn, we'd like to hear more about what

158

happened in that saloon. It's getting late. If you'd care to follow us, we'll see to it that you get something to eat and drink before you go on your way."

"Isn't necessary, ma'am."

"Don't call me ma'am. My name's Emma or Emmaline. Mandy makes you out to be a pretty interesting character—and says you have character, to boot. I'm not convinced, but the pot's on and I don't fancy eating alone. One thing about Buzzard. When he was home he livened up the place. It's gonna be mighty empty without him."

"Yes'm."

Emma shot him a reproving look.

"Uh, Emma, I mean. I'll be glad to sit at the table with you and your daughter."

Emma looked Gunn up and down. He shaded his eyes again.

"Oh, put on your hat, man," she said. "Hell, I've had enough formality for one afternoon. Mandy, you coming?"

Mandy broke into a smile as she looked at Gunn.

"I sure am," said the young woman.

Gunn walked past the women to the open grave. He looked down at the casket. It was covered with a shovelful of dirt, flowers, pieces of pine boughs. He heard the crunch of the women's shoes as they walked toward their buggy.

"Sorry, old timer," he said quietly. *"Vaya con Dios."*

The Mexicans came over as he was leaving.

"You are going to the house of the women?" asked one.

"I am."

159

The Mexicans exchanged glances.

"The young one is very pretty and very wild," he said, "but the older one is the hungriest."

"What do you mean?" asked Gunn.

The Mexican shrugged.

"Enjoy your supper," he said in Spanish.

CHAPTER SEVENTEEN

The Anderson house was a sprawling adobe that had been built with care. It stood on a hillside above the town, its log beams jutting from the walls, flowers and cactus plants well-tended, growing in profusion around the stone walkways. Gunn followed the buggy to the stables out back. He helped Mandy unhitch the horse that pulled the buggy, accepted her offer to put Esquire up. She watched him fork hay into the stall, pour out a coffee can of grain.

"Papa always talked about you," she said. "He said if it wasn't for you, the miners up on Grasshopper Creek would have had a far worse time than they did. Whatever happened to that Chinese girl?"

"Soo Li?"

"Yes. She was very pretty. Everyone said she went off with you, that you probably married her."

"She went off with me. She's dead."

Mandy drew back, shocked. The teasing tone vanished.

"I—I'm sorry."

"No need to apologize. She was a good woman."

Gunn slapped his clothes with his hat, beating dust out of the cloth. He looked at Mandy closely. She wasn't much younger than Emma. He took Anderson's widow to be only about twenty-two, twenty-three. Mandy was only about nineteen or twenty. She must have been about thirteen or fourteen when he was up on Grasshopper Creek.

"I didn't know your father," he said. "Leastways, I don't remember him."

They walked to the house together.

"Papa was a good man. Honest, hard-working. But he was crazy, too. About gold. And sad."

"Sad?"

"He knew it would never be as good again as it was in Montana. Oh, he liked it here. He loved the desert. But the gold just wasn't here. Not enough of it, anyway."

"Sometimes a man just has to keep looking."

She stopped, looked at him oddly.

"Why, that's just what Papa always said.

Mandy took him in the front door. The living room was spacious, cool. The furniture was polished wood. The decorations were all crafted out of natural things: wormwood, lava rock, potted cactus plants. There was a miner's pick and shovel on one wall, pictures painted on cloth, framed and hung quietly where there was too much empty space. Gunn wondered whether Buzzard spent much time in the room. Probably not. There wasn't much of him there. A woman had created it and the mining implements seemed to be only tokens to acknowledge Buzzard's existence.

"Make yourself comfortable," said Mandy, "I'll

162

change and be with you shortly."

Gunn wondered how the two young women got along. They seemed comfortable with one another, but there had to be some rivalry there. Soo Li had told him once that the character for trouble in Chinese writing was two women under one roof.

A Mexican maid came in, asked him if he wanted anything to drink. She was squat, fat, in her thirties. Her face was pretty, the cheekbones high, splashed with crimson that bespoke her mixed blood.

"Whiskey," he said.

"Emma will be here in a minute. I will bring the whiskey."

Emma came before the whiskey did. Gunn sucked in a breath when he saw her. She had changed to a light frock that was cut away at the bodice so that her breasts swelled up over the top of the material. She had her hair tied back with a pale blue ribbon that matched her eyes. She smiled at him.

"I hate black," she said. "I hate funerals."

"Me too," said Gunn, grinning.

The maid brought a bottle of good whiskey, three glasses, a pitcher of water. She set them on a low table in front of the massive divan.

"That will be all, Lupita," said Emma. "Please call us when supper's ready."

Lupita nodded, left the room quickly. Emma poured two glasses half full of whiskey. She lifted the pitcher of water, looked at Gunn.

"No, thanks," he said. "I'll just have it straight."

"Good. Buzzard has this whiskey sent down from Los Angeles. Have you been there?"

Gunn shook his head.

"It's an exciting place. I miss it. I miss the people, the fashions, the gossip."

Gunn took the glass of whiskey. Emma sat down, waved her hand over a place next to her. Gunn sat a foot away, closer than he would have wanted.

"You don't like it here?"

"I love it here. I just get homesick sometimes. I'm from Los Angeles. My father owns a ranch in the San Fernando Valley. I go there from time to time. Buzzard never liked it much. Civilization was the coward's way out, he used to say. I'll miss Buzzard. He was kind to me and to Mandy. He gave us our freedom, spoiled us."

"I didn't know him before," said Gunn.

Emma's eyebrows arched. She sipped her drink. Gunn did the same.

"Funny, but he talked about you as if you were an old friend. He certainly admired you and respected you."

"I'm grateful. But Buzzard was about to tell me something important. It had to do with a couple of men I'm hunting. Snake and Chigger. I think Buzzard knew who they worked for, or where I might find them."

She leaned back on the divan, crossed her legs. She had fine legs, smooth under the light silk stockings. She wore pretty blue sandals and her feet were pretty with delicate veins marbling the skin and her trim ankles.

"Did he tell you anything?"

"He started to say something. A name, maybe. It started out as 'Ol.'"

"That's all?"

"Yes. Does that mean anything to you? Olive, Olivia,

Ollie, Oliphant?"

"Oliver," said Mandy, coming into the room. "Oliver Miller. He runs the mercantile up at Julian."

Gunn pursed his lips, let out a low whistle. He kept coming up with that name. First, Lorelei had mentioned it and now Mandy Anderson. She walked to the table, poured herself two fingers of whiskey, drank it neat. Gunn's jaw dropped. Mandy wore a short skirt, sandals, a thin blouse that buttoned high but did not conceal her ample breasts. Her hair fell loose over her shoulders. Her skin was fair, the Swedish heritage apparent in her eyes and hair coloring.

"The name means something to you, Mister Gunn?" asked Emma.

"Maybe. I've heard it before. You know this Oliver Miller?"

Mandy poured herself another drink, filled Gunn's glass. She sprawled in a chair, her legs spread wide in a most unladylike manner. Emma never so much as blinked an eye. Gunn thought, *You can put expensive clothes on a girl like Mandy but she was still down home country.*

"Oliver Miller is a mouse," said Mandy. "A shopkeeper. I don't know how he could possibly have any connection with dangerous men like Chigro or Spivey."

"You know them?" asked Gunn.

Mandy tossed her head, sipped a generous mouthful of whiskey. Emma's eyes canted and she appeared to be mulling over not only Gunn's question, but Mandy's reaction.

"I've seen them around," said Mandy. She shot Emma a look. "Well," she snapped, "everyone knows

165

what kind of men they are. Oliver Miller would dirty his britches if Snake said 'boo' to him."

"Buzzard seemed to think there was some connection," said Gunn. "If that was the name he was trying to say. Does this Miller have any mining interests? Does he deal in stolen goods? Does he have a shady past?"

Both women laughed at once. Heartily. Gunn felt like a fool.

Emma dabbed at her eyes. The suppressed laughter continued to shake her.

"Forgive us for laughing, sir," she said, "but you don't know Oliver Miller. He's a—a little pipsqueak of a man who's afraid of his own shadow. Perhaps Buzzard was in his cups and just pulling your leg the slightest little bit."

Gunn's face darkened like a thundercloud. Buzzard had been drinking, but he was deadly serious when he leaned over the table and started to give Gunn a name. A name that meant something. Something important. Emma and Mandy were having their fun, but there was something odd about this Oliver Miller. Emma had called him a pipsqueak. So had Lorelei. Perhaps he was. But a pipsqueak could be controlled—by someone.

Suddenly, Gunn knew that Oliver Miller was an important key. Somehow, he had to find out what Miller's connection with Snake and Chigger was. And those two men were even more of an enigma than Miller. Lorelei had been raped by Snake. Mandy knew more than she was telling about the man. And no one, besides Buzzard Anderson, would even talk about the man. And yet they moved freely from town to town.

166

They robbed, they killed. One of them was a rapist. And they could control a town, shut it down, hogtie it like a thrown steer.

No, Snake and Chigger were just as small as Oliver Miller seemed to be. But behind them all, perhaps linking them together, was someone else. A powerful, shadowy figure who moved people around like checkers on a board. And somewhere in there was a man who bought up mining claims or stole them. C.O. Molinero who was the most mysterious of all.

"I'm sorry," said Emma, abruptly. "We've been rude to you. Have another drink, Mister Gunn. Lupita is preparing a wonderful supper for us. You'll stay to dine and let us make up for our indiscretions."

"Ma'am, I've had enough to drink, begging your pardon. You and your daughter don't mean any harm, but you have the advantage over me. I'm a stranger here and I'll probably get throwed and stomped a time or two yet before I catch up with Chigger and Snake. So I'd best be resting up in town before riding on to Julian."

"Not tonight, you won't," said Emma. "Right, Mandy. I don't think Ramona is quite ready for you so soon after my husband's death. And we'd really enjoy your company. But no more talk about those—those renegades. Let us show you the warm side of our hospitality, Mister Gunn. Please. As a boon to me and in memory of poor old Buzzard."

Gunn hesitated, then Mandy came close to him, put her arm around his neck. She kissed him on the forehead and her fingers tousled his hair.

"Please stay," she said. "It will be terribly lonely for

us without Buzzard. And Lupita really is a fine cook. Really, I wish she worked here full-time, but her father is a tailor and she does sewing for him three days a week. When we do have her, she's a treasure. You mustn't leave without sampling her food."

"Do stay," said Emma, smiling and toasting him with her drink.

Gunn looked up at Mandy, his complexion turning sallow. He gulped, swallowed hard.

"Well, I guess there's no big rush," he stammered lamely. "And I could use some grub. You gals have really blown my hat in the creek."

Gunn was more than a little drunk by the time supper was served. And he still hadn't asked Emma and Mandy about C.O. Molinero. But he had promised not to talk anymore about the men he was tracking. It seemed to upset them. The two women seemed bent on having a good time and remembering the man they had lost in their own way.

Mandy was tipsy when Lupita set the table with steaming dishes of *carne asada,* tortillas, *frijoles refritos,* delicately cooked squash, fresh fruit, cheeses and good California wine. She seemed to sober up with food in her stomach. She sat next to Gunn and her hand kept dropping into his lap, touching his leg. Emma, sitting across from him, slipped out of her sandles and ran her toes up and down his shins.

By the time coffee and fresh chocolate pie was served, Gunn was determined to go back into town. He had no wish to cause hard feelings between the two women. One had been recently widowed, the other had lost her father, but each seemed overly affectionate toward him. And he had Lorelei on his mind.

"We'll take our brandy in the living room, Lupita," said Emma. "Are you staying the night?"

"Yes, *señora*. I have a little sewing to do and I can take it to my father's shop in the morning."

Gunn listened idly to the two women talking, but he was thinking of the torn piece of fabric in his pocket. He had not looked at it since his sight had returned. But now was not the time.

"I'd better skip the brandy," he said, "and get on into town. I want to get an early start in the morning before the sun gets too hot."

"Nonsense. You'll stay the night," said Emma. "We have a lovely guest room. We'll not allow our guest to be turned out at such a late hour."

It was late. The meal had taken hours. He had drunk too much wine, too much whiskey. Still, the two women were a problem. Perhaps the liquor had made them behave so during supper.

"I won't refuse you, Emma, but I'll be leaving right early."

"Fine. Lupita, please bring a bottle of aguardiente, the fine brandy I brought from Los Angeles. Gunn, will you take my arm?"

"Mine, too," said Mandy quickly.

Gunn escorted the two women into the living room. The three of them swayed like sailors walking ashore after months at sea. Gunn sat between them on the couch. He drank the brandy, which was dry and smooth, chased it with black coffee that Lupita had

169

made up fresh. Even the coffee was without bitterness.

Sometime later, Lupita came in, said good night. Gunn didn't see her. Emma was embracing him, kissing him on the mouth. He struggled to move, but she had him pinned. Mandy was doing something to his trousers.

Gunn didn't know how the kissing had gotten started. There was some teasing, some poking. Then Mandy had smacked him. Then Emma. Just playful, at first. But now it seemed to have gotten serious. Mandy had his belt unbuckled and, unless he was mistaken, she was pulling his trousers off.

"Whoa, there," said Gunn, his tongue thick as a buffalo's, "you're getting a mite skittery there, Mandy. This ain't a pants-pulling party, is it?"

Emma breathed into his ear.

"It's any kind of party you want to make it, stud."

Her tongue lashed into his ear. Mandy jerked his pants off over his boots. Or had she taken off his boots earlier? Gunn's brain bobbed like a cork on a fogged-in sea. Emma was stripping him out of his shirt and there were too many hands to count any more. They all seemed to be touching him in different places, some of them unmentionable.

Then Gunn got the giggles. Maybe it was Mandy's tickling tongue on his loins, the inner slabs of his thighs. Or maybe it was Emma's mouth on his nipples. The sensation was an odd one and he didn't suppose anyone had kissed his tiny nipples before. He laughed so hard that he knew he had lost all control. He was naked, in a room with two playful women and he didn't give a damn if the creek rose or the well went dry.

170

He heard the whisper of cloth, opened one eye and saw Mandy peeling out of her frock. The sight of her bare breasts was as rare as the fur on a frog. She stood up, slipped her chemise down over bare legs and Gunn felt a tug in his loins. Emma, by this time, had moved on down to his sunken belly button and was probing that with her tongue. Gunn felt as if he was strapped to a lightning rod during a thunderstorm.

"Ladies, ladies," he pleaded, with no conviction whatsoever.

"You hush, you darling man, and let us take care of your needs." Emma moved down to his loins, began nibbling at his private parts. Gunn squirmed with a combination of delight and shyness. He felt a hand squeeze his hardening cock.

It was Mandy's. She had moved in and shoved Emma aside. Emma laughed, began to undress before him while Mandy stroked his throbbing stalk. Emma slipped out of her clothes as if she were on a stage, savoring his glances, turning and posing for him as she dropped each separate item on the floor. She slid her panties down her legs, exposing the dark thatch between her legs.

"I gather I'm in for a going-over," said Gunn. "Both at once?"

Mandy dove to his crotch like a kingfisher and swallowed his penis with one gulp. He felt electricity shoot up his spine. Emma smiled and peeled off her silk stockings. She hefted her breasts with both hands and walked toward him, slinking like a stalking cat coming in for the kill.

Gunn grabbed a handful of Mandy's hair, drew her

away from his crotch. She slid over his body, wrapped her arms around his neck and kissed him hard on the mouth. He tasted salt and lemon, his own juices. Emma straddled him, guiding his bone-hard cock up to her sex-cleft. Mandy girdled his belly, rocked to a coital rhythm while peppering him with hot, wet kisses.

Emma sighed as she slid down his pole, burying his manhood deep in her loins. Gunn felt a swift surge of pleasure as he burrowed into the smoldering sheath. Emma pushed up and down, sliding him in and out. Mandy turned to watch.

"Emma, you are a caution. Don't use him all up."

"Oh, we're doing just fine, aren't we, Gunn?"

Gunn made an inhuman sound. He could barely breathe with Mandy's weight on him. Emma pumped up and down until her eyes rolled in their sockets and her mouth went slack. She cried out as the first orgasm rippled through her body. She quivered, her hands gripping his thighs, the fingernails digging in like talons.

"Ooooh, Emma, you did it," whispered Mandy. "My turn."

"Wait, again, again," said Emma. She moved slightly and climaxed another time. Gunn struggled to rise up. He was sliding from the divan.

His butt hit the floor and he went down all the way. His neck was bent against the divan. Mandy got off of his belly and pulled Emma away from him.

"Don't hog him all for yourself," she teased.

Emma pulled on Gunn's feet, dragging him out into the center of the floor. The rug burned his back.

"Take him, sweet," said Emma, panting. Her body

glistened with sweat.

"Gachhh," said Gunn.

Mandy slid atop him, squirmed until she found the right position, then reached down and thrust him upward inside her. He slid through the tight, gripping lips of her cleft and sank into brothy heat. Emma leaned over him so that he saw her upside down. She dangled her breasts over his mouth, swaying them from side to side.

"Kiss my nipples," she demanded huskily.

Gunn drew one of her nipples into his mouth and suckled the gristly nubbin.

Mandy bobbed up and down on his swollen rod, her hands flat on his belly. Her eyes glazed over with a rapturous madness.

Gunn fought to concentrate. His alcohol-laced brain, the two women, his tiredness, all served to disorient him. Mandy bucked with a series of shattering climaxes. Emma smothered him with her breasts. He was both blind and ravaged. His body surged with pleasure, but his intellect sagged like a deflated balloon. He felt as though he was a prisoner, without will or freedom. He rebelled against that. With all his heart he rebeled against it. And even with the shrouds of whiskey, wine and aguardiente blanketing his will, he rose up, roaring, a gentle savage waking up in a righteous rage.

He shoved Emma away from him, then half sat, pushed Mandy off her peg-perch and rolled away from them.

"Listen, ladies," he rasped, "I'm calling a godamned recess. I'm as horny as either of you, or both of you put

173

together, but I can't service the pair of you while I'm flat on my back. Now if you've got a soft bed here, let's see what you're made of—separate or together. And I'll ride the bronc to the end. But damned if I'll let you both take my scalp when I can't even see who the hell is getting all the satisfaction? Clear?"

The women, both disheveled as bantam hens in a roost full of cocks, looked at him with wide owl eyes.

Then Emma began to chuckle softly.

Mandy giggled inanely.

Gunn sighed with resignation and threw up his hands in exasperation.

"Damn," he muttered. "Are we all plumb loco or just stone drunk?"

Emma sobered, briefly.

"Both," she admitted. "It's just that you're a man such as we haven't seen before, Gunn. Buzzard talked about you so much, built you up so much in our minds, spoke of how ladies chased you and broke their hearts over you that we had to find out for ourselves. Yes, the bed. A big bed for the three of us. I still want to see what you're made of."

"I know what he's made of," said Mandy, in a far-away voice, her eyes staring at nothing. "I want him inside me so bad I could just scream."

"I guess Buzzard was right about one thing," said Emma, her voice laden with that same dreamlike quality as drenched Mandy's tone, "you have had some experience with women."

Gunn looked at them both. Both beauties. Both agonizingly wanton and desirable. He wanted them. Individually, or in tandem. He wanted them and his body throbbed with the driving pulse of his blood.

"Experience?" he asked. "Well, I guess I've seen the elephant and heard the owl—but you two take the cake."

"And the berries?" said Emma, crawling towards him.

"Yes, damn near," he gruffed. "Now, which one of you wants to be first—in bed?"

CHAPTER EIGHTEEN

Gunn woke up sometime before dawn. It was dark as a coalbin in the room and it took him several moments to get his bearings. There was only one body in the bed besides his own. Mandy, he judged, from the feel of a breast. She made nose and mouth sounds that told him she was deep in sleep.

Where was Emma?

She had been the hungriest, after all.

Gunn dressed quickly in the dark. His tongue had furred over and his throat was raw as a scraped shinbone. He had worked most of the alcohol from his system. The women had done that. Mandy would, he knew, if he touched her, turn in her sleep and present herself to him. She was young, full of energy and what could probably be called lust.

Gunn didn't have an ounce of lust left.

He carried his boots in his hand, opened the door. A feeble light glimmered from somewhere in the back of the house. He padded toward it. He smelled coffee. He needed coffee.

Emma was there, sitting at a table. The kitchen was enormous, festooned with ladles, pots, scrapers, whisks, spoons, pans, hanging from hooks attached to the log beams. The wood stove was big, too. Coffee bubbled and steamed in a pot. The counters were clean, the floors, the stove—everything neat and orderly.

"Good morning," she said, her voice pitched low, still husky from sleep. But her face was scrubbed and her hair tied back in a tail with a ribbon. "I'll fix you breakfast, if you like."

"Just coffee. I hunt better on an empty stomach."

"Who are you hunting, Gunn? What are you hunting?"

Her eyes accused him twin flashes of understanding, with a raking dip of eyelashes.

He sat down, screwed on his boots. He ran fingers over his face, felt the scratch of his beard.

"Chigger, Snake, and a man named Molinero."

"Molinero?"

"C.O. Molinero. Ever hear tell of him?"

Emma got up, poured coffee in a pair of cups. She set one before Gunn, sat down. The coffee smelled rich; the steam curled upward, aromatic as morning itself.

"Ah, so you've heard of our mystery man. Buzzard wanted to know the same thing. It drove him. Molinero, you see, moved in on one of Buzzard's claims. Buzzard hadn't filed properly, but before he could do anything about it, Molinero took title under the name of the Julian Mining Company."

"Did he find out who Molinero was?"

"No, and those who asked too many questions disappeared. Were never seen again."

Gunn blew on his coffee. It was still too hot to drink.

177

"You mean Buzzard didn't find out anything?"

"Oh, he found out Molinero was a Spaniard, an aristocrat, apparently. They say he has fair skin, blue eyes, and is very, very rich. He may live in Julian or San Diego. Or both. He is also known as 'John Smith.'"

Gunn's eyes narrowed.

"Ring a bell?" asked Emma, wryly.

"Two men killed Freddie Waite. Sometime after that, they were joined by a man calling himself Smith. John Smith. But no sign of him. Or of the other two for that matter."

"What about Kimmons and Torres? You never did tell me about them."

"They're dead."

"Did you . . . ?"

Gunn nodded, sipped the hot coffee.

Emma shuddered.

"There's more to you than meets the eye," she said, ladling a spoon in her coffee, blowing on it to cool. "I can see why Buzzard talked about you so much."

Gunn could learn no more from Emma. But as he formed a picture in his mind of those he was seeking, the beginnings of a plan began to form. Emma had said that people who got too close to Molinero had a habit of disappearing. The man couldn't stand heat. Well, Gunn made a decision to push Molinero. To make him sweat. Bring him out in the open. And at the same time, perhaps, flush out Chigger and Snake.

He saddled up Esquire just before dawn broke. In the stable, a sound startled him.

He wheeled, his hand hovering near the butt of his pistol.

"Don't shoot me," said a woman's voice.

Gunn stepped out of the shadows, saw Lupita standing just outside the door.

"Oh, it's you. Sorry."

She went to a stall, led out a small horse. She put an old Mexican saddle on the animal.

"You are leaving?" he asked, as he slapped Esquire on the rump to get him moving out of the stall.

"I will ride to Julian," she said, "to the house of my father. I have finished sewing to give to him."

She stepped away from her horse, lifted a carpetbag, showed him a jacket. It was small, but had an expensive weave. The jacket was gray and black, a herringbone tweed, finely tailored.

"See?" she said, "you cannot tell where it was torn." She opened the jacket, showed him the inner hem where she had taken a piece of matching material, then trimmed the rest so the theft wouldn't show. Gunn was impressed.

"Where did you get that?" he asked.

"Why, from my father's store in Julian."

"Do you know the owner of this jacket?"

"No. But my father might."

Gunn reached in his pocket, pulled forth the scrap of material he had ripped from one of his attackers when he had been blinded. He held it up to the jacket.

Lupita's eyes widened.

"Why, it's the same material!" she exclaimed.

"Exactly," said Gunn. "How'd you like a companion to ride with you to Julian?" He swung into the saddle.

"Let me tie my bag to the horse and I will ride with you," she said. "I think that material you have is from the place of the tear on the jacket."

"So do I," said Gunn, "and I aim to find out who

179

owns that jacket."

"Be careful," she said. "Julian is full of secrets."

Gunn wanted to say more, but she finished tying her bundle to the saddle and mounted up. She rode on ahead, down toward the gate. Emma stood on the porch and waved. Gunn waved back, then prodded Esquire to catch up. Lupita was already galloping toward Ramona, filling the dawn air with a fine dust.

Gunn knew something was wrong long before he reached Ramona. Lupita rode ahead of him, too fast. It took him awhile before he realized that she didn't want him to catch up to her. He tried to recall their conversation, piece together what might have upset her. All he could figure was that it had something to do with her father and that damned coat.

Yet why hadn't she said anything at the time? She hadn't shown him any white flag. Maybe she was one of those quiet ones, with the Indian blood, who kept everything inside, everything hidden. He tried to picture her face when he had talked to her, but it had been dark and he had not seen her features clearly.

He rode past a cluster of rocks, expecting to see Lupita's horse on the long stretch ahead. The road was empty. Lingering dust tickled his nostrils. He slowed Esquire, stood up in the stirrups. The sun rose reluctantly on the horizon. The dust settled. The road twisted, rose up through more rocks, brush. It was hellish country and a hellish time of morning to track someone.

But he didn't need to track Lupita. He knew where she was going with that jacket. To Julian. And that's where he was going. To find the men he was seeking and have a talk with Lupita's father.

And then he remembered he didn't know her last name or her father's name.

But someone did.

He spurred Esquire. There was no hurry now, but he wanted to keep pressing those he sought. In Ramona he would start to leave wide tracks.

Let them come for him. For he would surely go for them.

"Mister, you don't want to know the answer to that question."

"Why?" asked Gunn.

"Because it ain't healthy to even ask about anyone named Molinero."

Gunn eyed the alderman with a frosty stare.

"I'm asking anyway."

The alderman stood on his porch in his undershirt and a hastily donned pair of trousers. Gunn had gotten Oren Rossiter out of bed a few minutes ago while the sun was peeling off the morning haze. It had taken him a half hour or so to find out the names of the city fathers and he had already asked two others the same question: Who and where was C.O. Molinero?

"Even if I knew, I wouldn't tell you."

"Somebody knows."

"Who are you, anyway? You bent on going to your own funeral?"

"The name's Gunn. I've already talked to Sideman and Fuentes."

"And what did they tell you?"

Gunn cracked a smile.

"You go to Julian. Talk to a man named Martinez. I don't say he'll give you the answer to your question, but if anyone can, it's him."

"Martinez? Where would I find him?"

"Pedro Martinez. He's a tailor. Got a big shop on Juniper Street. He does harness work, too."

"He any kin to Lupita?"

"You know some things, don't you, Gunn? Lupita's his daughter, but you stay shy of her. She won't give you the time of day on Molinero."

"How about Chigger and Snake? You know them?"

Rossiter's face drained of color. He turned on his heel, went through the door. Then he stopped, looked morosely at Gunn.

"Mister, you done asked one question too many," Rossiter said. "If you got close relatives, you might want to write them a goodbye letter."

"Much obliged," said Gunn, grinning. He tipped his hat, mounted Esquire and rode out of the yard. Rossiter stood in the doorway a long time, scratching his thick sideburns, rubbing his forehead.

Gunn didn't have to see anyone else. Rossiter had been more helpful than he realized. He now knew where to find Lupita's father and it was a pretty good bet that Martinez knew Molinero. Beyond that, Rossiter had as much as admitted that Chigger and Snake were part of Molinero's bunch. He had already guessed as much, but Rossiter's reluctance to talk about those two went a long way toward confirming Gunn's hunch.

He had already spent too much time in Ramona. The sun was climbing the horizon, changing from a glaring red globe into a distant orange flare that was too bright to gaze at directly. Esquire jumped to the spurs. Twenty-five miles or so down the road, Gunn was sure he'd find the answers to all of his questions.

Lorelei reined up when she heard someone call her name.

Oren Rossiter stepped away from the entrance to his dry goods store and stood at the hitchrail until Lorelei turned her horse and rode toward him.

She was dusty, hot, and her horse was sleek with sweat. It was early afternoon and she had not stopped since leaving Anthony Smithers' office early that morning. She had hoped to catch up with Gunn but had not seen his horse anywhere in Ramona.

"Oren," she said, looking down at him.

"You wouldn't be after finding a man maned Gunn, would you?"

"Why, yes, I am. Have you seen him today?"

"He woke me up this morning. I heard he spent the night with Buzzard's widow."

Lorelei fought to retain her composure, but her face darkened at the news.

"Why are you telling me this?"

"Because he's stirred up half the town with his questions about Molinero."

"Is he still here?"

"I doubt it. He was bent on going to Julian. I know he's after your father's killers, but he's just going to get himself a pine box."

"Then he went to Julian?"

Oren preened his sideburns, wiped his hands on his

canvas apron.

"Like a bat out of hell."

"What did you tell him?"

"Too much, probably. I told him about Martinez."

"The tailor?"

"Yes. Lupita's father. But someone else was asking about him, too. Two men rode through about an hour ago."

"Who?"

"Bounty hunters. Woolhoyt and Davis. They showed a poster around, rode out of here on fresh horses. I'd say this Gunn has himself in a heap of trouble. Was I you, I'd stay shy of this jasper."

"You're not me," Lorelei said tightly. "Thanks for the information." She reined her horse hard. Oren took a step toward her.

"Wait," he said, "there's more. Chigger and Snake rode through here early this morning just after I opened up. They didn't stop and they had blood in their eyes."

Lorelei nodded, dug her spurs in her horse's soft flanks. The animal bunched up its muscles and bounded forward. Oren Rossiter shook his head sadly and watched her ride off.

"Everybody's crazy," he said to no one. "Every damn body."

Gunn rode Esquire into the shade of the livery barn, dismounted. He led the horse inside, nodded to the smith who was working over some tack in a corner.

"You got some time?" Gunn asked.

"In a minute or two." Then he looked closely at

Gunn's eyes and stood up. "I reckon I can set this aside."

"Walk him for ten minutes, strip him, rub him down, grain and water him. I want him saddled and ready to ride in thirty minutes."

"Hell, mister, that horse is plumb dripping. Ought to rest him for a day at least."

"I don't have a day. How much?"

The smithy scratched his balding head. Gunn fished out some bills, peeled off four of them.

"If there's more due, I'll pay you when I get back. Thirty minutes, friend."

"Yes, sir. Yes, sir."

Gunn handed him the reins and walked into the sunlight.

"Now there goes pure trouble," said the smithy to Esquire.

Gunn strode across the street, looking up at the large sign on the false front.

"JULIAN MERCANTILE," read the legend. And, underneath, the name, "O. Miller, prop."

Two doors down, he read another sign, hanging in a window.

"Handy," he said.

The other store legend said, "P. Martinez, Tailor."

CHAPTER NINETEEN

Gunn walked into the mercantile store, glanced around as his eyes adjusted to the light.

A few people browsed among the yard goods. A man stood before a display of hardware. Lupita peered out from behind a bolt of cloth standing on a table. Next to her was a small, thin man, dark-haired, brown-eyed, in his thirties. A pencil jutted out from behind one ear.

"Lupita," said Gunn, striding toward her. "Long time no see."

Her face fell.

"Go away," she whispered loudly. The small-statured man suddenly grew nervous.

"I'm looking for Oliver Miller," said Gunn.

"What do you want?" asked the man next to Lupita.

"Are you Miller?"

"I am." The voice was high-pitched, faintly accented. "Who are you?"

"Don't talk to him," said Lupita to the storekeeper.

"The name's Gunn."

"I—I'm Oliver Miller," said the man. His hands

started to shake.

A thought crept into Gunn's mind. It had been back there, lurking, hidden, but now it took form. He wondered why he hadn't realized it before. It was a long shot, but it might prove out to be the strongest clue of all. Gunn's eyes swept the bolts of yard goods. He walked over to one, picked it up, threw it on the table.

As Miller watched, Gunn unrolled a foot or so of the material. Then he reached in his pocket, pulled out the swatch of cloth he had torn off one of his ambushers. Lupita watched him with wide, staring eyes, eyes that glimmered with fear.

Gun threw the torn swatch of cloth on the table near the unrolled material.

The herringbone matched.

"Are you Spanish?" he asked Miller in that language.

"N-no," said Miller, and Gunn knew he was lying.

"I am looking for the man whose coat this piece of cloth came from. If I don't get the answer here, I'll talk to your father, Lupita. Now what's it to be?"

Lupita gave a short cry and started running. She knocked over the bolt of cloth she had been examining and before Gunn could stop her, raced by him.

Miller backed away as Lupita ran through the front door and disappeared.

Gunn debated about going after her, but knew that such an act would cause him more trouble. A man chasing a woman down the street would be frowned on in all but the most liberal towns. Besides, he had Miller on the defensive.

Gunn stalked the shopkeeper, backed him into a corner. The people in the store stared in their direction.

The man looking over the hardware had a hammer in his hand. Gunn shot him a look to discourage him from mixing in.

"Miller," said Gunn softly so that his voice wouldn't carry, "you have about three seconds to start answering my questions. If I don't like your answers, I'm going to start shutting off your air." Gunn made a menacing shape with his hands. "Savvy?"

Miller nodded. His face twitched with a nervous tic.

"Now, where can I find C.O. Molinero?"

"I—I . . ."

Gunn stepped closer. The man with the hammer walked over, still curious.

"Friend, if you want to buy that hammer," said Gunn, "just take it over to the counter and count out the man's money. Otherwise, you and I are going to tangle and you'll be wearing that hammer permanent."

The man gulped, drifted away. The women saw what was happening and scurried out of the store.

"Spit it out, Miller. Molinero's place. Where does he live?"

"Th—there is a hacienda west of town. A wide road to it. But let me go there first. I don't want any trouble."

"You or someone already has trouble. John Smith. You know him?"

Miller shook his head.

Gunn put his hands on the man's shoulders. His grip tightened. Miller began to shake all over like a man with the shivers.

"That name is sometimes used by—by . . ."

A shadow filled the door.

Gunn whirled, crouched. A man stood there, a pair of pistols hanging from his gunbelt. A Mexican, lean as

188

a whip. A man Gunn had seen before, from a distance.

"You don't have to tell the gringo a damned thing," said Chigro.

Gunn stepped around a barrel filled with axe handles, into the open.

Then a woman screamed, burst through the doorway. Chigro twisted to face her.

"Don't, Chigro!" shouted Lupita.

"Get the hell out of my way, woman!"

Lupita looked desperately at Gunn, made up her mind. She started running toward him.

Gunn opened his mouth to shout a warning.

Chigro went for his guns. His hands were supple, delicate blurs. His fingers grasped the butts of his pistols with a loving swiftness. The leather of his holsters whispered with sliding sounds as the pistols became part of his hands.

Gunn dodged out of Lupita's way, hoping to get her out of the line of fire.

Oliver Miller gasped. He wet his trousers, shrank away from the threat of violence in the air. Embarrassed, he cowered, covering his crotch with his hands.

Gunn's hand streaked for the Colt .45 in its sheath. His eyes locked on Chigro's across the room. He already knew he would be too late, but death is decided in fractions of seconds. Lupita blocked his vision even as his pistol cleared leather. His thumb cocked the hammer back with a sudden automatic action as his target disappeared behind a frantic Mexican woman's back.

Chigro squeezed the twin triggers of his Colts. The revolvers bucked with explosions, spouted flame and lead.

Lupita didn't have a chance.

She staggered as the soft balls of lead thunked into her back, driving flesh before them, splintering bone, shattering veins until blood gushed from the holes like crimson fountains.

Gunn, unable to fire, watched in horror as fist-sized holes appeared magically in her chest. Her mouth opened in a silent attempt to scream. She lurched toward him, stretching out her arms, her eyes pleading with him to save her from certain death.

He didn't hesitate. He ran toward her, grabbed her. He put his arms around her, fired at Chigro, even though he knew his aim was a trifle off. Still, his ball caught the Mexican bandit in the hip, spun him around.

Chigro staggered as Lupita and Gunn went down, the weight of her driving him back. He had no chance to hammer back, but Chigro wasn't having any more of it. Pain twisted his features, blunted his senses. Blood drenched his legs. A shock ripped through his body, numbing his hands. He reeled through the doorway, instinct driving him to retreat, tend to his wound.

Gunn's mind raced with a frantic thought.

Where was Snake?

The woman in his arms shuddered, made sounds that wrenched at him. He lay his pistol down, turned her over. Lupita's eyes stared at him fixedly.

"It hurts," she whispered through a throat bubbling with blood.

"I know. Hold on, Lupita." The bullets had caught her high in the lungs, missing the heart, giving her a few more minutes, or seconds, of life. Gunn turned to the quivering storekeeper.

190

"Get whiskey and a doc," he barked. "Move! Fast!"

With a shriek of bewildered anguish, Miller managed to head for the door.

Behind him, Gunn heard a sound.

He twisted around, saw a drape move. He ducked down, picked up his pistol. Without thinking, he cocked it and fired three quick shots into the drape. Then he dragged Lupita behind a table, waited. He reloaded quickly, filling all the empty cylinders until the six were ready.

A silence settled inside the store.

Had he hit anyone? Was that Snake coming up behind him? It would figure that Chigger and Snake would try to take him that way. One in front, one in back. It was a stacked deck. But it hadn't worked. Not yet.

Lupita made a sound. Gunn looked down at her, safe for the moment. Where in hell was that whiskey? Did they have a doctor in Julian?

"Don't try to talk," said Gunn.

"No. Must. Listen."

Her voice was barely audible. He bent down to hear her words They came slowly, painfully, with little breath behind them. And each time she spoke, blood bubbled up in her throat, gushed from her wounds.

Gunn felt her life ebbing away. A wave of tenderness crept over him. He didn't know the woman, but she was a living creature and she deserved to live out her days. She had seen Chigro outside and had come rushing in to prevent him from shooting a man she hardly knew. Why? Was she concerned about him, or about Chigro?

"Watch out for Snake," she said. He heard the whistle of death in her speech.

"I will. Don't talk about it. You're bad hurt, Lupita."

"You good . . . man. Chigro . . . he loco some. Husband."

"What? Chigro's your husband?"

Lupita nodded.

Gunn sobered. Thoughts flashed through his mind. No wonder she had ridden away from him back in Ramona. It was hard to imagine a sensitive, hard-working woman like this married to a renegade, an outlaw, but he had seen such things happen. He had known women who were attracted to men who were on the wrong side of the law, who treated their wives or their girlfriends like so much prairie sod.

"Cuidado con la mujer. Molinero. *Cuidado."* Lupita gasped to say the words in Spanish. Gunn held his ear close to her mouth to catch the words.

"Quien?" he asked.

Lupita sucked in air and her throat gurgled like a sink hole after a flash flood.

He rubbed the sweat off her forehead, held her tightly. She was dying and he was powerless to save her. He silently cursed the fate that had made her come to this place when Chigro was out for blood. Suddenly, his thoughts shifted to the man he had shot in the hip. He remembered his own wife, Laurie, and her senseless death.

Chigro had to pay for this. He had to pay for killing Lupita. And Freddie Waite. At least, for those two. Perhaps for many others. It was no longer a matter of a promise made to a dying man. Lupita did not deserve this pain, these last agonizing moments of life. She did not deserve a man like Chigro.

"Go to the rancho Molinero," she sighed. Gunn

could barely hear her. She said something else that sounded like "via." Was she asking him to go away? Va via meant that. Or was she trying to tell him the way to the rancho?

"Who is John Smith?" he asked.

"Juan Molinero. He is the father of . . ."

Just then Miller came back with two other men. They had whiskey and brandy. One of the men knelt, looked at Gunn, then at Lupita.

"Querida," he said softly, *"que te pasa? Ojala que . . ."*

"You are her father?" Gunn asked.

"Yes. This is very bad." He kissed his daughter, hugged her. "Let me hold her now. Are these her last moments?"

"Yes," said Gunn. "Perhaps you will want to bring a priest."

"They have sent for the padre at the mission. She has a child inside her. Did you know that?"

"No," said Gunn, but that could have explained her chubbiness. His jaw tautened as his teeth locked in rage. He slid Lupita into her father's lap, took a bottle of whiskey from Miller's hands.

Lupita shook her head when he brought the bottle up to her lips.

Pain had altered her features, smoothed out all the wrinkles, taken away the red earth color of her cheekbones, bleached out the dark, leathery tan of her face. He touched her hand and it was cold, nerveless. He looked at Pedro Martinez and shook his head. Tears rolled unashamedly down the man's cheeks. Gunn stood up, holstered his pistol. He looked at Miller.

"You," he said, "stay. I'll be back after I've tracked

Chigro. We're going to the Molinero ranch."

The other man with Miller opened his mouth.

"You will not have to track Chigro far, *señor*. He is at the Cantina Escobar across the street. He is drinking a lot of whiskey and is trying to stop from bleeding too much."

Gunn looked at the Mexican who had spoken. He stood there, his hat in his hand. He was not trembling, not afraid.

"Who are you?" Gunn asked.

"I am working for the jefe, Martinez. I sweep and do the carpentry."

"Was Snake over there, too?"

"I do not know. I do not think so."

Gunn turned, knelt by Lupita. He kissed her on the cheek.

"*Adios,*" he said to her. "*Vaya con Dios.*"

"She has already gone," said her father.

Gunn strode across the floor. He did not look back. He saw only Chigro's face as the man had fired into his wife's back. He wanted to put him down bad.

But where the hell was Snake?

CHAPTER TWENTY

The two men knew what they were doing. First, they rode slowly through town, checking the hitchrails. They were headed for the livery stable when Gunn stepped out of the Julian Mercantile.

Jerry Woolhoyt spotted him first. He made no outward sign. Instead, because he was a professional, he smiled at Gunn and spoke quietly to his partner without moving his lips much.

"Comin' out of the mercantile, Randy. Our man, looks like."

Randy Davis, who had been looking on the opposite side of the street turned slightly in his saddle, regarded Gunn.

"That's him," agreed Davis.

The men stopped their horses, wheeled them into position.

Gunn saw them, read their faces. The long shadows of late afternoon striped the street, daubed the buildings. Bounty hunters. Their dusty clothes, their bearing, the way they looked at him, jockeyed for position, told him who they were. He froze, figured his chances.

"It's dead or alive, Gunn," said Woolhoyt. "Your choice."

Davis started his move. Not much choice, at that. Woolhoyt's right hand started edging toward his own pistol. No choice at all. They were going for the kill.

Gunn, his senses honed fine, didn't have to think. He was going to have to go through these two in order to get to Chigro. And these two were professional—all the way.

The tall, gray-eyed man gave no sign. He didn't crouch, or move from his position. He had a clear killing space for each man. Only his hand moved. It moved like a diving hawk, one moment motionless, the next streaking for the butt of his Colt.

Davis saw the blurred movement, knew he had waited too long. Woolhoyt, too, saw that they would have to hurry.

Gunn's pistol, melded to his hand, slid from the leather. His thumb expertly cocked the single-action Colt. He swung it, brought it up shoulder-high, Davis steadied in his sights, his head in perfect alignment with the blade from sight, the rear buck horn. Gunn didn't hesitate. He squeezed the trigger, felt the pistol kick up. He brought it down, cocking with his poised thumb.

He couldn't see Woolhoyt through the cloud of white smoke, but Gunn knew where he was. He held steady, fired again.

Woolhoyt's pistol was out of the leather, solid in his hand. He felt puzzlement as he heard the second explosion come so quickly after the first shot. Davis

196

was already pitching out of the saddle, a hole just above the bridge of his nose. Just a hole, no blood.

Gunn ran, at an angle, to get around the smoke. He crouched. Woolhoyt's pistol exploded. The air sizzled with the buzz of the bullet. Woolhoyt coughed as Gunn's bullet plowed into his gut, just below his rib cage.

Woolhoyt reeled from the impact. He seemed to be looking for his target when Gunn shot him again. The bounty hunter's head exploded like an overripe melon dropped from a great height. The .45 ball struck him just above the left temple, flattened and altered course. Splinters of bone and a spray-cloud of blood, as fine as dust, spewed from the exit hole on the right side of his brain.

Gunn watched the man's eyes roll up, lock in a death stare. He hammered to half-cock, worked the plunger. Empty hulls spit out the gate as Gunn twisted the cylinder. He shoved two fresh bullets in even as smoke continued to drift lazily out of the barrel.

He walked past the dead men toward the Cantina Escobar. Davis lay sprawled in the dirt, his mouth open, crammed with dirt. The hole in his forehead turned blue-black at the edges and there was only a thin rime of blood at the entrance. Woolhoyt was drenched with blood and his neck had broken from the fall. His body still twitched although the man was dead.

People gawked from concealed positions. Gunn checked them all as he stalked toward the cantina. He carried the Colt at the ready. It was cocked.

He stopped outside the cantina, listened.

The street was silent as a tomb.

197

"Chigro?" Gunn called. "Either you come out or I'm coming in."

"Fuck you, gringo."

Gunn's blood froze. He would have to go in.

He looked around. The horses owned by the bounty hunters stood riderless, their reins hanging to the ground. Good horses, ridden hard. Not much left in them. But enough. Gunn walked to them, picked up their reins. He led them to the side of the cantina. He hoped what he planned to do would work. If not, he was going to be shot stone dead.

Her jerked the reins, started running past the open door of the cantina. He heard something click from inside the bar, but no one shot at him. As the first horse's head reached the doorway, Gunn turned, shoved the other in behind him. The horse balked and Gunn rammed the barrel of his colt deep in its flank. It kicked up at him, but bolted on inside. The neighing was deafening.

Close on their heels, Gunn dashed through the doorway, crouched low.

Chigro started firing. The horses screamed in terror.

One horse staggered from a bullet in its neck. Gunn saw the orange flame, the smoke. Behind the white cloud, Chigro leaned against the bar, firing as fast as he could cock and pull the triggers of his pistols. The air filled with flying lead. Bullets ricocheted off the adobe walls of the cantina. Splinters of wood exploded from the doorway.

Gunn ducked under the other horse, fired at Chigro. He saw the man's legs twitch.

"Hi jo de la chingada!" hissed Chigro.

His guns went silent as the hammers thunked on spent shells.

Gunn stepped in close, shooing the horse away. The other one had gone to its knees, blood streaming down the broad expanse of its neck.

"This is for Freddie," said Gunn, squeezing the trigger.

Chigro stiffened as the bullet plowed into his abdomen. He glared at Gunn with the pain-crazed ferocity of an animal.

"And this one is for Lupita." Gunn cocked slowly, fired.

Chigro screamed in agony as the bullet smashed into his genitals, mashing the soft flesh to pulp. The Mexican doubled over in pain, then slid to the floor. His pistols dropped from his hands.

"Ay de mi," sobbed the bandit. He looked up at Gunn, the hatred flaring like coals in his eyes.

"And this one, you sonofabitch," said Gunn, "is for me."

Gunn shot him in the belly. Dust puffed up from the man's shirt and spread with blood.

"Kill me, you bastard," groaned Chigro.

"I want you to die real slow, Chigger. I want you to think about why you're dying. I want you to think about hell."

"Chingado. Cabron."

Gunn walked over to the wounded horse, fired a bullet into its brain. He shooed the other one out of the cantina, took one last look at Chigro.

The man was still alive. He stank of death. His life leaked from his wounds and made little rivers in the sawdust on the floor.

"Adios," said Gunn softly, and stepped through the door.

He reloaded as he walked toward the livery barn. He shoved the Colt back in its holster and watched faces bob out of sight as he passed.

"I'll have my horse now," he told the smithy. "Owe you any money?"

"Not a penny," said the smithy. "How many'd you kill anyways?"

Gunn took the reins, led Esquire out into the fading light of afternoon.

"Not nearly enough," he said.

The Molinero ranch lay at the end of a straight road through shadowed hillocks bristling with rock and vegetation. The adobe was whitewashed, the yard neat. He saw no one, but a pair of horses were hitched to a post a few yards from the house. They looked fresh, unridden. Oliver Miller rode a few feet in front of Gunn. The man had not stopped shaking. Gunn felt sorry for him, but he had no sympathy for the man beyond that.

Gunn and Oliver Miller dismounted. They tied their horses to a standing hitchrail. Gunn shoved Miller ahead of him, walked warily through the patio to the archway. The door was just beyond, massive, expensively carved. He lifted the iron knocker, pounded it three or four times.

The door opened.

The woman was very beautiful. She stood there, per-

fectly poised, dressed in riding togs that looked to be
especially fitted for her. Her hair was black, hung long
over her shoulders. Her eyes were like the dark berries
of August and her skin was light and without blemish.
She wore silver earrings and a beaded silver necklace
that drew the eyes to her neck, her chest, the breasts
that pushed against the light blouse she wore. She was
the spitting image of Oliver Miller.

"Oliver. You've brought Mister Gunn with you."
She glanced down at her twin brother's trousers,
sniffed. "You must bathe and change clothes, my
brother. What will our guest think?"

Oliver sheepishly went inside. Gunn followed the
woman to an expansive living room. It was cool and
colorful. The furniture was massive, the wood studded
with ornate brass nails.

"I won't sit down and I won't have a drink," said
Gunn as Oliver scurried on into the bowels of the
house.

"You were offered neither," she said curtly. She
looked so tiny, so delicate.

"You must be Olivia Molinero."

"You have figured it out, then." It was a flat state-
ment.

"Most of it. What's your first name? Carmen?"
She laughed, tossed her head. She strolled to the
fireplace, put a booted foot up on the hearthstone.

"Consuela. I compliment you, Mister Gunn. You
have come further than any one else."

Gunn knew he was talking to C.O. Molinero. He had
figured part of the name out before. Oliver Miller.
Molinero meant miller in Spanish. But who, then, was

John Smith. Lupita had as much as said that this was their father. But where was he? And where was Snake Spivey?

"You must have schemed a long time to pull this off. Set your twin brother up in business, use others to do your dirty work. But it's all over now, little lady."

"Oh?"

"Chigger's dead. So is Lupita, I'm sorry to say."

Olivia's eyebrows arched. Her face started to blanch before she recovered her composure.

"Is . . . what about . . ." she stammered. Then she clamped her mouth shut. Gunn felt the hackles rise on the back of his neck. Olivia was too small to wear the coat Lupita had repaired. So was Oliver.

He had missed something. Somewhere along the way.

"Your father here?" Gunn asked casually.

"My father has been dead for many years. The gold fever gripped him. He died trying to get it and when he did, the gringos took it away from him. Did you not know that? No, of course not. They don't talk about Molinero. They don't want to admit that he is dead. That they killed him. They say he is still alive and lives out here as a hermit. But they know the truth. They killed him and hid his body so that we could never give him a proper burial."

The bitterness of her words knifed into Gunn's brain.

"So, it's revenge and you want the gold you think your father should have had."

"Yes," she hissed and Gunn knew that she was mad. Insane. Her eyes glittered like a hunting snake's and he knew that she was capable of cruelty and murder in the

name of justice. He shivered to think what she had
done in retaliation for a wrong done her father.

He started to say something when there was a
commotion at the front door. Gunn turned, too late.
Pedro Martinez came into the room. He was dressed
differently now. He wore the herringbone suit and a
wide-brimmed hat. He carried twin pistols, pearl-
handled, nickel-plated.

"So, you have figured it out, eh, Gunn?"

"Now, I do, John Smith. Your daughter tried to
protect you. She lied."

"Lupita was a good daughter." He shifted his gaze to
Olivia. "It is time," he said. "*La Culebra esta afuera,
listo.*"

"*Malo!*" Olivia barked.

Gunn clawed for his pistol.

Martinez didn't draw. He tilted both pistols up,
cocked them. Gunn knew he would never make it. The
tailor had him beat going in.

Then Olivia shouted a warning.

"Look out!" she screamed.

Martinez whirled. Gunn had time now. His pistol
snaked out of the holster. He cocked, fired as Martinez started to shoot Lorelei, who had burst into the
room. Martinez staggered as the ball slammed into his
back. His knees buckled. His pistols boomed, the
barrels pointed at the floor.

"Lorelei!" exclaimed Gunn.

Then something slammed into his back. Olivia shot
by him. Lorelei tried to grab her, but the smaller
woman eluded her. Gunn recovered, shoved his pistol
back in its holster.

203

"What's going on?" asked Lorelei.

"She's getting away. Snake's outside waiting for her. Quick!"

Gunn had understood Martinez when he spoke in Spanish to Olivia. He had said Snake was outside, ready to ride. *La Culebra.*

Olivia had disappeared.

Outside, Gunn and Lorelei saw Snake throw a rifle to Olivia. Lorelei and Gunn drew their pistols at the same time.

Snake pulled his pistol, took aim as he cocked.

"You get her," said Gunn quickly. "Snake's mine."

Guns exploded. The air filled with smoke, the stench of burnt black powder. Bullets whined. Olivia went down as Lorelei fired twice. Snake looked as if an unseen hand had jerked him from the saddle. He went down, blood gushing from his chest.

Gunn raced forward. Olivia was alive, but just barely. Lorelei's shots had both been true. Two holes pumped blood from the woman's chest. Very near the heart. From the way the blood was spurting, Gunn figured Lorelei's bullets had struck an artery.

Spivey tried to sit up, shoot Gunn as he walked over to him.

Gunn shot him between the eyes. Snake fell backward, his eyes staring at nothing. Gunn reached down, ripped off his shirt. He wanted to be sure.

The tattoo was smeared with blood, but the eagle was there, perched on the cactus. And under one of its feet was a writhing snake.

Oliver Miller rushed to his sister, took her in his arms. She still gripped the rifle. He rocked her gently.

sobbing uncontrollably.

"I'm sorry for what has happened," he said in Spanish.

"*Me voy,*" she said. "I'm going."

Olivia gave a sigh and then stopped breathing. The blood slowly stopped gushing from her wounds. Then Oliver gave a horrible, stifled cry and snatched up the rifle. Before Lorelei or Gunn could react, he shoved the barrel in his mouth and pulled the trigger.

Lorelei screamed and turned her head away.

Gunn cursed silently.

"Poor bastard," he said, "that was probably the only act in life he's ever done on his own."

Gunn put his arms around Lorelei. She shivered.

"Smithers do you any good?" he asked.

"Yes. Does it make any difference now? They're all dead."

"Isn't that what you wanted?"

"Not like this. It—it's horrible."

"Be on guard about what you want," he said softly, "you might get it."

Gunn walked away from her, slowly unwrapped Esquire's reins.

"You're leaving?"

"Going north. There were bounty hunters after me. There'll be more. It's best this way." He climbed into the saddle. He could hardly see her as the sun smothered itself in the sea. The shadows were deep now, shrouding the dead as if they were already in their graves.

"I—I'll come looking for you," she said, her voice sounding far away.

"Someday," he said, "maybe I won't be running any-more."

He turned Esquire and rode into the north, into the darkening night.

When the nightbirds flew, it seemed to him that he could hear Lorelei out there somewhere, calling his name.

THE CONTINUING SHELTER SERIES
by Paul Ledd

#13: COMANCHERO BLOOD   (1208, $2.25)
A vengeance seeking U.S. Cavalry officer is on Shell's trail—and forcing him straight into a Comanchero camp of the meanest hombres in the West. The only soft spot is Lita, and the warm senorita's brother is the leader of the Comanchero outlaws!

#14: THE GOLDEN SHAFT   (1235, $2.25)
A captivating lady, who happens to own a gold mine, may be a lead to the man Shell's tracking. Before the gunsmoke clears, Shell has helped his lady friend save her mine, gets his man, and does a little digging in the shaft himself!

#15: SAVAGE NIGHT   (1272, $2.25)
Shell's leading a gang of down-and-dirty banditos into a trap—that holds a surprise for Shell as well! A savage chieftan's untamed daughter is about to welcome Shell south of the border!

#16: WITCHITA GUNMAN   (1299, $2.25)
Shelter's on the trail of an outlaw bandit who's leading him into Indian territory—where a savage buffalo hunter is keeping a woman as his slave, a woman *begging* to be rescued!

BOLT BY CORT MARTIN

#9: BADMAN'S BORDELLO (1127, $2.25)

When the women of Cheyenne cross the local hardcases to exercise their right to vote, Bolt discovers that politics makes for strange bedfellows!

#10: BAWDY HOUSE SHOWDOWN (1176, $2.25)

The best man to run the new brothel in San Francisco is Bolt. But Bolt's intimate interviews lead to a shoot-out that has the city quaking—and the girls shaking!

#11: THE LAST BORDELLO (1224, $2.25)

A working girl in Angel's camp doesn't stand a chance—unless Jared Bolt takes up arms to bring a little peace to the town . . . and discovers that the trouble is caused by a woman who used to do the same!

#12: THE HANGTOWN HARLOTS (1274, $2.25)

When the miners come to town, the local girls are used to having wild parties, but events are turning ugly . . . and murderous. Jared Bolt knows the trade of tricking better than anyone, though, and is always the first to come to a lady in need . . .

Available wherever paperbacks are sold, or order direct from the Publisher. Send cover price plus 50¢ per copy for mailing and handling to Zebra Books, 475 Park Avenue South, New York, N.Y. 10016. DO NOT SEND CASH.